An End...

Book 3

By

Theresa Shaver

Sun and Smoke, Book Three of Endless Winter

Copyright © 2018 Theresa Shaver

Print Edition

All Rights Reserved

Cover art by Melchelle Designs

Contents

Chapter One...Skylar

"AIRIA? AIRIA, I need help!"

I repeat her name again and again but there's no response. I'm so focused on getting an answer from her that I don't even realize that the gunfire has stopped until hands grab the back of my jacket and haul me to my feet.

The communicator is ripped from my hands and I follow it with my eyes as it's passed to someone who's just walked up.

"I'm sorry, Skylar. AIRIA is no longer under your control. She belongs to me now."

The words hit me like a Mack truck. No, no that's not possible. AIRIA's mine! She's my mom and my dad and all I have left of them. No one can *take* her from me! Who the frack does this guy think he is?

I lift my eyes from the unresponsive communicator in his hands up to his face and stagger back a step.

"Uncle Bill?"

He's older and his face is harder than I remember, but it's him.

He gives a sharp nod. "Hello, Skylar. I was sorry to hear that your father is no longer with us. He would understand what will happen now. I've brought my people to take back what I loaned him so long ago. AIRIA is now under my complete control. Your authorization has been reduced to a red level but you don't have to worry, I will continue to shelter you for the sake of my friendship with your father. You just won't have any more authority in my bunker."

I should be happy to have a small part of my family show up but I don't know this man. All I know is that he's just taken away the only real parent I have left. He can't seriously just cut me off from her like that. Can he?

I'm not going to get an answer from him now because he nods at the guy holding me and motions towards a Hummer that's pulled up on the other side of the car barricade. The guy doesn't shove me towards it but his grip on my shoulders is forceful so I have no choice but to move toward it. I struggle against him, trying to see what these invading soldiers are doing with my friends. That's what they are, invaders and no matter who that man was once, I have a feeling in my gut that he's now going to be my biggest enemy. I manage to catch a glimpse of Rex, Lance, and the others being hauled to their feet with their hands tied in front of them before we make it to the car barricade. As I scramble over the hoods of the double rows of cars between me and the Hummer, I turn my body sideways so I can watch my people being herded towards some kind of troop transport that had breached the barrier. The fight goes out of me when I see them being loaded into it. If these soldiers were going to kill them they would have done it here, where countless bodies litter the parking lot.

I wait docilely for the soldier to open the Hummer's door and climb in without a word. Uncle Bill stated that the bunker is his now so that must be where we're headed. That works for me, Benny is there and the sooner I have my hands on him the better. I'm surprised to see two other people in the back seat with me. A boy and girl that are both around my age stare at me as the door slams closed, sealing me inside with them. I don't know who they are but they both wear the same uniforms as the other soldiers so I dismiss them and turn to look back out the window to try and catch another look at my friends.

"Skylar? Do you remember me?"

My head swings back to the boy who has spoken. Who is this guy and how does he know my name? I just stare him down and wait to see what he wants from me.

"Uh, I'm Jackson…Bill's son."

I squint my eyes to see if I can see anything of the boy I had met once before long ago at a ruined birthday party but there's nothing, so I slide my gaze past him to the girl who's scanning me with a creepy amount of interest. I look back to Jackson for a half a beat and shake my head before turning my back on both of them with a parting shot.

"Sure, ruining parties seems to be your thing."

He stammers out a few words of apology but I just tune him out and study the soldiers running around the parking lot collecting weapons off of dead bodies. The flames from the hotel have caught in all three wings, turning night into day, so I see the transport truck my friends were loaded on move out. I wish Uncle Bill would hurry up. I have a lot of question for him and I want AIRIA back!

When I hear the driver's side door open I look over with impatience but it's just some random soldier who fires up the vehicle and pulls away. I guess I'll have to wait for my answers. Jackson tries talking to me again but I just hold my hand up between us. I have no interest in speaking to this boy until I have hashed things out with his father.

As we leave town, I catch sight of the road where we had left my dad's truck before we snuck into town. I wonder if these guys have found it or if it will stay down there, hidden.

I let my mind drift to all that's happened in the last few months after going so many years with just me and Ben and the same old routine. We went from so many years alone to being surrounded by people and finally finding the ability to trust again and make plans to for the future to now being invaded by soldiers and not knowing anything about what is in store for us. I can only hope that Uncle Bill has plans to work with us on our plans to start rebuilding and planting crops. Depending on how many soldiers he has with him, we could get a lot accomplished.

All thoughts of working together leave my mind as the girl lets out a soft gasp. I turn to look out the windshield and gasp myself. There are floodlights set up all around the clearing where Rex's people had camped before I let them into the bunker. But what sends my blood racing is the lines of people on their knees with their hands behind their heads. It has to be every single person from the bunker out there on the ground as men with guns guard them. I look in every direction ahead and see fences being unrolled around the edges of the clearing and huge tents being erected against the rock wall. What the frack is going on?

As soon as we come to a stop behind the transport ahead of us I claw at the handle of my door and let out a screech of frustration when I find it locked. My furious eyes swing to Jackson causing him to lean away from me as I hash out the order through my grit teeth.

"OPEN...THE...DOOR!"

He leans back further practically laying on the girl beside him. It's her that nods to me before addressing the driver.

"Private! Unlock the doors, please. Miss Ross would like to reunite with her little brother."

I pin the girl with a hard stare. How the frack does she know that? How does she know anything about me? She just gives me another nod at the sound of the locks clicking open so I spin away and throw the door open. I'm halfway across the clearing scanning faces of the people on their knees when I give up and start screaming his name. I hear his small scared voice call my name and zero in on the area it came from. I only manage a few more feet towards him when a gunshot rings out and a divot of dirt goes flying into the air right in front of me. I throw myself to the left and drop to the ground as screams fill the air from the scared people in front of me.

There's so much noise as people scream and soldiers shout but no more bullets fly so I roll over, push myself to my feet, and look behind me. I see Jackson pull a rifle away from an angry soldier as the girl barks orders to stand down at the others. I push myself to my feet and just stare at them all in disbelief. Why would they shoot at me? What threat am I to them that they would shoot so randomly at a girl looking for her brother?

I feel a small body crash into me and it almost sends me back to the ground again but I manage to brace myself enough to stay on my feet.

"Sky...Skylar! They yelled at us and made us all leave and said we can't live inside anymore cause it's theirs now! They're all really mean! AIRIA...AIRIA won't even talk to me anymore and the ceiling, the ceiling out here is too big!" He sobs against my side as I wrap my arms around him.

I hold him close as I turn in a circle and see Belle and Matty starting to rise up as well as all the other people who had flattened themselves to the ground when the shot went off. I keep turning and see Rex, Sasha, Lance, Ethan, and Marsh being shoved our way. Then I see Jackson and the girl a few steps away from me. Jackson looks like he's ready to apologize again but the girl just looks grim. When I see Uncle Bill stride up to join them, I feel the fury boiling up until it spews out.

"What the FRACK is wrong with you? Lining up women and children on their knees and shooting at them? What are you, some kind of MONSTER?"

He glares back at me but doesn't bother responding. I catch movement out of the corner of my eye and glance that way to see the girl slowly nodding her head as if to say, "Yes, he is."

Interlude 1
AIRIA EAST
Seven Years Ago

Jackson

"I can't believe we're stuck here! We could be at the pool right now. I hate year-round school!"

I catch the small ball I'm bouncing against the opposite wall of the hallway we're sitting in and glance over at Joslin to see if she agrees but her black curls act as a wall, covering her face while her small fingers fly over the tablet's keyboard. I nudge her with my shoulder causing her to whip her hair away from her face as she shoots me an impatient look.

"It is what it is. Get over it! I just need a few more minutes and I'll be into their network, then we can snoop around."

I let out a sigh as she turns back to the code that's flashing over her screen. I know she'll ignore me now until she hacks into the network here. She sees every private network as a personal challenge to her hacking skills and this one being military is the big shiny golden ring.

I lean past her to look down the hall to see if any of my classmates are moving but everyone is still sitting in boredom along the walls as we wait for my dad to show up and give the class a tour of the base. As far as school field trips go, this is one of the worst as far as I'm concerned. It's bad enough dealing with my father on his scheduled visitation weekends without Mom there as a buffer, but now I have no choice but to listen to him all day droning on about how military discipline is the be-all and end-all of success. I decided a long time ago that military life wasn't for me, especially if it turns people into the hard-ass my dad is.

I throw the ball again and again and chew on my lip. I know if Dad has his way that in two years I'll be sent to a military school and the choice will be taken from me. I shudder at the thought of that and vow to keep working on

Mom to stop that from happening. I fumble the next catch when Joss hisses.

"Yes! I did...WOAH!"

I crawl over to retrieve the ball and settle back beside her but the weird look on her face has me glancing down at the screen of the tablet she's clutching. There's an angry red banner flashing on it.

"Oh! Did you get busted?"

"What...no. I just broke into their Wi-Fi, I didn't steal nuclear launch codes!" she says with a shake of her head.

I laugh. "I'm pretty sure that we don't have anything nuclear in this country."

She gives me a flat look. "You know what I mean. I don't know what's going on. Something weird is happening though."

I look down the hall at my bored classmates and see my teacher Ms. Hudson tapping her foot in impatience while glancing repeatedly at her watch. My dad, who's always a stickler for being on time, is late. That alone tells me that something's going on. This part of the base is where the public would come to sit in for lectures or wander through the displays that they have on the history of Canadian military so there's no one around for me to ask what's going on. I laugh to myself. Maybe I'll get lucky and I won't have to spend the next hour listening to my father tell everyone in my class how amazing it is to be a soldier and it's the one thing of importance that everyone should do in their life.

I'm just about to start throwing my ball again when a door slams open at the end of the hallway, catching my attention. I can just see a flashing red light before the door slams behind my father who is striding towards my teacher. He gives her an annoyed look as she rushes towards him before glancing down the hallway at my fellow classmates and then zeroing in on me. He holds his hand up towards my teacher to stop her chatter and barks my name.

"Jackson, front-and-center!"

I scramble to my feet and pull Joss up with me, maybe he won't ream me out if I have an audience. Just as we reach him, I hear him telling Mrs. Hudson that the lecture will be delayed and that she should put all of my classmates in the lecture hall where he will join them shortly. He holds me back when I move to join my classmates and waits until they've all left the hallway before he turns to me with a stern look.

"Come with me. Something's happened and I need you to follow me right now!"

I glanced over at Joss but she looks just as unsure as I feel. She starts to edge towards the door to the lecture room so I reached out and grab her arm and hold her close. I don't want to face whatever my father has in store for me alone.

My father gives her an annoyed look when she stays by my side and barks at her. "Go with the rest of your classmates. This doesn't concern you!"

I hold tight to her arm and shake my head in denial. For once I'm going to defy him.

"No! She's staying with me. She's my best friend and I'm not going anywhere without her."

His face turns beet red in anger but before he can bark at us again, a soldier runs up to him and says in an urgent tone, "General, we have to go!"

My father turns back to us and throws up his hands. "Fine, bring her but you both need to keep up and do as you're told."

We rush to follow my father and his aide deeper into the base through twisting and turning corridors that flash with the red emergency lights on the ceilings. We finally make it to the end of a long corridor where a double set of elevators doors wait open for us. As soon as the doors close I turn to my father and ask what's going on and why are the red lights flashing? I can see he's about to dismiss me once again so I ask again in my bravest voice.

"Dad, what's going on?"

He looks at me and then to Joss before finally sighing in annoyance.

"There's been some troubling developments. Nuclear bombs have been launched in the Middle East and Europe and we're expecting them to start heading our way shortly. We have a contingency plan for this sort of thing and we're heading there now."

My mouth drops open in shock and I stutter out, "Bombs? Nuclear bombs? We're going to be bombed?"

He nods his head yes. "I expect the bombs to hit North America within the next hour. We have an underground bunker that we're going to travel to where we will all be safe but I need you to listen to me and follow my exact orders. I'm not kidding Jackson, you must do exactly as you're told. This is serious!"

I can only nod my head in stunned belief but then an even scarier thought races through my mind.

"Dad! What about Mom? Is Mom coming? Did you call her? We have to get Mom. She has to come and be safe with us!"

His face goes completely blank at my panicked questions before he finally responses with a tiny shake of his head.

"I'm afraid she's too far away Jackson. She would never make it here in time. I'm sorry, there's nothing I can do to help her."

I can hear Joss gasp out a sob beside me as she realizes that her own parents will be left out in danger as well. I step back away from my dad in the cramped space and glare at him.

"Let me go. Let us go. We want to go! We want to go back to Mom and to Joss' parents. We don't want to be here with you!"

He looks at me with disdain and shakes his head. "That's not going to happen. You will be with me now and you're both going to have to toughen up. This IS reality! It isn't going to be for the next week or even the next month. Only the strong will survive what's about to happen and what the world will be like in the years to come. You both need to accept that this is happening whether you want it to or not!"

I angrily scrape the tears from my face before spitting at him. "You didn't even call, did you? You didn't even warn her what's coming! You're just going to leave her out there to die!"

My father is saved from answering me when the doors behind us open and he pushes both Joss and I out onto a concrete platform with an underground train parked beside it. I'm distracted by the lines of soldiers that are calmly entering the doors down the length of the train and settling in the seats. I shake my head in amazement as my grip tightens on Joss' hand. I had no idea there was a train underneath my father's base.

I'm scared and all I want to do is run with Joss back to the elevators and up to the ground level so that we can try and get to our families before the bombs start dropping. Sadly, that's not going to happen as my father hands us off to his aide who pushes us into the train and down into a seat. As soon as we're seated Joss yanks her hand from mine and pulls out her tablet. Her little fingers start flying over the keyboard faster than I've ever seen them move before.

I watch the soldiers filling up the seats on either side of us in stunned disbelief for a few minutes before I turn my attention to what Joss is doing. I can see that she has her email open and is typing out a message.

Without looking up she asks, "Would your mom know where this bunker is?"

I shrug my shoulders. "I don't know, she might. He might have told her about it before they divorced."

She just gives me a curt nod and continues typing before she finally hits the send button.

The determined expression that had been on her face leeches away as she slumps back against her seat and her lower lip starts to tremble. She's back to being a scared ten-year-old girl instead of the fierce hacker she wants to grow up to be.

"What did you do?" I ask her in a small voice.

She lets out a trembling breath and swipes her hand underneath her damp nose.

"I still had a weak Wi-Fi signal down here so I managed to get a message out to my mom telling her what's going on and asking her to contact your mom so that they can know where we are. I don't know if they'll get it in time but at least I got to say goodbye. I'm sorry I couldn't send one to your mom. I don't know what her email is."

She looks down the length of the train car at all the serious looking soldiers and asks in a defeated voice, "Where do you think they're taking us? And why couldn't he bring the rest of the class with us? There's got to be room for them on this train? Do you really think he just left them up there to die when the bombs drop on us?"

I try and suck back the tears that I want to let loose as I shake my head.

"I don't know. He can be a real hard-ass sometimes but I can't believe that he would just leave them up there to die. This must just be a precaution or a drill of some kind."

I look around again but I don't see anybody who looks anything other than afraid and don't believe my own words.

We're jolted in our seats as the train lurches and then starts accelerating down the tunnel. Joss looks down at her tablet and sighs. "Well, there goes the Wi-Fi. We are now officially cut off from everyone we ever knew."

We sit in silence holding hands in the dark as the train picks up speed and heads to somewhere that is supposed to protect us but all I can think is if this is the real thing then who's going to protect us from my dad?

Joslin

I take a deep breath and suck back the sob that wants to climb up my throat. I'm tougher than this. I've spent my whole life being bounced from one foster home to another, never knowing where I'm going next. This is just one more time that I have no control over my fate.

The problem is, I finally landed in what I thought would be my forever home two years ago. After years of being shuffled from one house to another, I was finally handed over to the Dubois'. It was the first time I didn't feel like I was only in a house so that my foster parents could collect an extra check every month. They actually seem to want to get to know me - my thoughts and my feelings and my opinions on things. I've never experienced anything like it before in my whole life. They are warm and caring people who work from home as computer programmers and one of the first things they did was teach me how to use electronics, something no one had ever given me before.

When they started teaching me the basics of coding, it seemed like my brain just came alive for the first time. It was a rush and I loved every minute of it. They gave me the gifts of acceptance and unconditional love.

It took me a while to trust them but once I finally let my guard down, we became a family and with the adoption papers filed a few months ago I started calling them Mom and Dad. Now I was going to lose them. Back to being alone again with only this boy beside me.

Because of the conditions I had lived with, in multiple foster homes, I'd had to learn how to deal with all types of bullies from adults to other children. When I started at the school where Jackson attended, he was one of the first people to single me out and not in a good way. He would make fun of my curly black hair and the way I would use it to screen my face whenever I was nervous.

I knew that he would just keep at me if I didn't do something so one day at lunch when he bumped into me on purpose I took the bowl of spaghetti he had on his lunch tray and dumped it on his head causing the entire room to laugh at him. For some reason instead of hating me for it, he ended up liking me and took the time to get to know me. It feels like he hasn't left my side since that day.

My hand's gone numb from how tight Jackson's been holding it. It's like he's using it as a lifeline but that's okay because I'm holding on just as tightly to his. I use my other hand to wake up the tablet laying on my lap and see that we've been traveling for just over 45 minutes. I don't know how far we've come but this train is moving faster than any train I've ever been on before so we could be anywhere from 100 to 300 kilometers away from the base by now. As I'm trying to calculate possible distances to figure out where we're going I feel the train start to slow. Wherever it is we're going, apparently, we've arrived.

I lean forward and look down towards the compartments ahead of us and see lights starting to blink on. It looks like they are making their way down to us. I think I can hear a computerized voice coming from one of the other compartments but the rest of the soldiers are making noise as they moved to stand so it drowns out whatever is being said.

The General's aide waves us to our feet and clamps a strong hand on both of our shoulders. It looks like he plans to hold on to us to wherever we're going. As much as I don't like being pushed around there's something comforting about having an adult taking us where we need to be. We step off the train onto a concrete and rock platform that is a mirror image of the one where we started our journey. There are lines of soldiers forming up to enter stairwells and two sets of elevators. Our guardian steers us to the lines to enter the elevators. The strangest thing is the lack of voices.

There have to be at least two hundred or more men and women around us but no one is talking. I look around at the faces and see plenty of fear but not one person is voicing it. The silence keeps me from asking all the questions rolling around in my head. I learned a long time ago that you could learn more with quiet observing than rambling questions. People tend to overlook kids if they're really quiet and sometimes will say things without thinking about the small ears nearby.

I'm nudged from behind as Jackson tugs on my hand so I look forward and step into the huge freight style elevators. He keeps giving me uncertain looks but all I can do is shrug. I'm along for the ride just like he is. It only takes a few minutes before the doors open again and we step out. My mouth drops open in shock at what I see ahead of us.

The space in front of us is massive. I look up to the high roof and see that it's a rock cavern and follow it with my eyes for at least the length of a football field or more. It's filled with double-stacked bunks from one end to the other.

My eyes well up with tears at the thought of living here surrounded on all sides by soldiers day and night. I suck the tears back. Not that long ago, I could fit all my belongings into a black garbage bag and privacy was a foreign concept I had only dreamed about. Living with the Dubois' has made me soft and I have a feeling that I won't make it here for long if I don't get my armor on.

"Donnelly, front and center!" Is barked from our left and we all turn towards Jackson's dad standing nearby with a clipboard waiting for us. When the aide pushes us in his direction, I finally get to know our babysitter's name.

As we move in his direction, I take another look at the men and women setting up the bedding on all the bunks that fill the room. I just can't believe that this is going to be my new home.

Jackson

I have a thousand questions I want to pile on my dad but he's busy ordering his men all over the place and I know better than to interrupt him. As soon as the last soldier moves away from him I open my mouth to let loose, but his aide, Donnelly, beats me to it.

"Sir! Where would you like me to take the children?"

Dad's face goes blank for a moment like he had forgotten about us and then turns dismissive with a small shake of his head.

"Take them to the officer's quarters. I don't have time to deal with them right now. I'm needed in the command center."

As he turns away from us, I reach out and grab his arm.

"Dad! You can't just stick us in a corner out of your way! We need to know what's happening. Please, Dad, I'm scared."

He looks down at my hand on his arm with a scowl before looking at me and then Joss who has tears streaming down her cheeks. His face softens briefly before firming back up.

"Listen, I know you're both confused and scared but things are happening fast and I need to be in the command center. This whole place is run by an artificial intelligence named AIRIA. I'm going to voice imprint both of you and give you a yellow clearance level. That means when you get to your quarters, you can ask AIRIA some questions and she will answer you." He scrubs at his face and glances over his shoulder in the direction he wants to go before sighing. "That will have to do for now. I promise once things settle down, we will have the conversation you want about your futures." He gives a curt nod to Donnelly and strides away without a backward glance.

I watch him walk away with sadness and anger. I'm furious at him for once again not caring about me or my feelings and saddened because he's all the family I have left now. I'm jolted out of my thoughts when a computer voice rings out above our small group.

"Jackson Mallor, voice print recognition complete. Access level yellow. Unidentified adolescent female, please state your name and birthdate for voice print recognition."

Joss's eyes lift to the high ceiling for the source of the computer voice before looking at me in confusion. I just shrug so she hesitantly speaks her name and birth date.

"Joslin Frost, voice print recognition complete. Access level yellow."

I have no idea what any of that means but don't have time to ask because Donnelly steers us deeper into the cavern, past the rows of bunks and through a set of double doors that lead to a hallway with offices off of it. He finally finds the door he wants that has yet another hallway with open doors. I look into the rooms and see living areas in each one before we reach the end of the hall and he motions us into a much bigger room. It has a small kitchen and living room with two open doors that lead into bedrooms.

I turn to ask him a question but he just holds up his hand and mutters, "Don't leave here." And shuts the door in my face.

I fume in anger and give the closed door a hard kick before turning away from it. Joss is standing in the middle of the living room with her tablet clutched to her chest as her eyes dart from each area of the room before settling uncertain eyes on me.

"What do we do now?" she whispers.

I shrug because I'm just as lost as she is. I throw myself down on the plain couch and look around the room that is going to be my home for the foreseeable future. It has none of the touches of home and it makes my heart ache for my mom.

I wonder what she's doing right now. Does she know what's happening? Is she scared? I feel tears well up and shake my head. This can't be right. I can't accept that I'll never see her again, that she's going to die out there all alone without me. This is all my Dad's fault! All he had to do was call her and she could have driven this way to join us. I spring to my feet in a rage.

"ARGGGGG! I HATE HIM!"

Joss flinches at my scream and takes a step back, her grey eyes wide and scared. She turns away and drops down on the couch with her tablet still clutched like a shield to her skinny chest. Seeing my tough, no-nonsense friend like this drains the rage from me and I plop down beside her.

"Joss, are you ok?"

When she doesn't answer me, I sigh and study her face. She looks like a small, scared trapped animal with haunted eyes that keep darting from place to place. She shouldn't be here. I did this to her.

"Joss, I'm so sorry! I should never have forced you to come with me!"

Her eyes finally land on me in confusion. Her voice is a croak when she speaks.

"What? What are you talking about?"

I look down with shame. "I grabbed you and told my dad that you had to come with us. If I hadn't of done that then you might have made it back to your family. I'm sorry."

Her grip on her tablet finally loosens and she reaches for my hand.

"So I could die too? Jacks, if what your dad said was true, then everyone out there is going to die. You saved my life by bringing me with you!"

I look up at her and give a half smile before asking, "Do you think he's telling the truth? Do you believe that the world is really ending?"

She gives a tiny shake of her head. "I don't know but I think we need to find out."

Joslin

I look up at the ceiling for any speakers and when I see one in the corner I ask, "Uh, computer, uh, AIRIA?"

"Joslin Frost, how may I be of service?"

I send a quick look to Jackson and when he nods encouragingly I continue.

"Umm, what's happening outside?"

"Joslin Frost, the current temperature is twenty-four degrees Celsius with scattered cloud cover."

I make an annoyed face at the answer and shake my head. "No. I meant, are there really bombs dropping?"

"Joslin Frost, current satellite imaging shows one thousand eight hundred and forty-four ground strikes have occurred worldwide."

I can't help the gasp that leaves my lips and I feel tears swell in my eyes again. I swallow hard and ask the question I fear the most.

"Have any bombs dropped close to us? Like, Ottawa?"

"Joslin Frost, no strikes have been detected in that area."

A breath of relief flows out of me. They're ok, so far.

"Um, if Ottawa is hit by a bomb, how far would the effects go? Our parents live in Stittsville. Would they be hurt?"

"Joslin Frost, Stittsville is approximately thirty-six kilometers southwest of Ottawa and would not be impacted by an initial blast. Prevailing winds blow from the west which would push the majority of the fallout away from that area. However, should there be strikes on Toronto, Kingston, Montreal and Quebec City, there would be an overlapping effect that would blanket the entire southern section of the

province. Secondary harm from the resulting EMP would also cause massive damage to infrastructure with the loss of electricity. Would you like a more detailed analysis?"

I shake my head but another thought jumps into my head with the news that my family might still be ok.

"No thanks. Umm, do you have an internet connection?"

"Internal network connection is available but an external connection requires a higher authorization level than your current standing."

I grit my teeth in frustration and grind out, "I just want to check my email!"

"Joslin Frost, higher authorization level is required for that function."

I want to throw my tablet at the speaker but clutch it close to my chest instead. It's the last connection I have with my parents and I think I might need it in the future. Instead, I ask, "Will you let us know if or when a bomb hits in our area?"

"Joslin Frost, I will provide updates as they occur."

My shoulders slump and I turn to Jackson, surprised to see a smile on his face.

"What? Why are you smiling?"

He lifts one shoulder in a shrug. "You heard it. They're still alive! They can make it!"

I squint my eyes at him. "Make what?"

"Your email! You told them what's happening and when we were going. As long as they get a hold of my Mom, she can probably bring them here!"

I bite my lip as I consider this.

"But you said you didn't know if she even knew about this place? How will they find us if she doesn't know where we are?"

He snorts out a laugh. "You don't know my dad! There's no way he wouldn't have bragged about this kind of place to her. At least, before when they were happy together. You wait and see! They'll show up here. I'm sure of it!"

I turn away and stare at the speaker for a minute before addressing the computer.

"AIRIA, can you notify us if our parents show up outside?"

"Joslin Frost, request for notification of perimeter breach noted."

I nod, satisfied for now. When things shake out as they will in the next few days, I'm going to see just how deep into this computer system I can get.

Jackson is dumping out his book bag and muttering about not having some of his possessions for the apocalypse until he comes up with his lunch bag. He sees me watching him and nods towards my own bag.

"We might as well enjoy our last real word lunch while we wait for my dad. It's got to be better than any of the food we'll get in here!" At my confused look, he smirks. "Trust me. I've eaten army rations before on our father, son, bonding camping trips. Cardboard and sawdust are the main two flavors and I can't even describe what powdered eggs taste like!" He gives a mock shudder and opens his lunch kit.

I have zero appetite right now so I mindlessly watch him eat while my fingers randomly tap the edges of my tablet. My mind is going in a million different directions about our situation and what it will all mean for me and my family. I play the game of what ifs until I'm ready to scream. Finally, I can't take sitting here one more minute so I jump to my feet and start pacing. I've only managed to do two circuits of the room when the ground under my feet heaves. It's not enough to throw me off my feet but it causes me to stagger and all the dishes in the kitchen clink together. I throw my hand out towards the wall and feel the trembling coming from it. My eyes snap to Jackson's and I see the same fear I feel mirrored in them.

"AIRIA! What's happening?" he yells out.

"Jackson Mallor, the cities of Toronto, Ottawa and Montreal have taken direct strikes. Yield unknown at this time."

I give up on standing and let myself fall to my knees. I can feel the tremors through my legs and just lower my head with my eyes closed. After the lonely life I've led, I don't believe in God, but I can't help but pray to him for all the people who just died.

Jackson

My mind is so overwhelmed at what's just happened that it goes blank. I can't process the idea of those three cities and all the people that lived in them just wiped off the map like they never existed. I'm staring at the carpet between my feet with the forgotten sandwich I had been eating dangling limply from my fingers when the door flies open. For a split second I think it will be my dad, coming to comfort me but of course, that's just a childish fantasy. He's never given me comfort before so why would the end of the world be any different.

Donnelly stands in the doorway out of breath as his eyes track from me to Joss on the floor. When he sees that we're both without injury, he gives a curt nod to us.

"Stay down for now. We are perfectly safe in here but we might have a few more jolts."

I can see he's about to turn and leave so I push to my feet.

"Hey! Where's my father? Shouldn't he be the one checking on his only kid?" I ask, heavy on the sarcasm.

The man frowns at me before turning to go. "He's a very busy man."

The door swings shut leaving Joss and me alone again. I spit out the worst curse word I know and then turn to Joss. She's on her knees with her eyes closed but I can see tears leaking down her face. I feel so helpless that I just want to punch something but I know there's no point in that. Instead, I step over to her and pull her to her feet. When her eyes open and meet mine, I still have no words to fix any of this so I just say the first thing that pops into my head.

"Come on, let's get out of here!"

Her eyes flare wide in shock so I wave a hand. "No, I mean out of this room. I can't just sit here and…wait. Wait for what? My dad? The start of the rest of our lives? Forget it. If he wanted us to sit tight in here then he should have kept the babysitter on us, right?"

She slowly nods her head and a spark of life glimmers into her eyes.

"Yes, if we are going to be stuck here then it's only fair we should get to see our new home. Let's go!" She grins.

We race to the door but I hold up my hand to wait as I crack it open and use one eye to scan down the hallway. When I see the coast is clear, I swing the door the rest of the way open and we slink down the hall to the end past the other rooms. From the silence, I can tell that there's no one else in any of the living quarters but the next hallway has offices and I can hear scattered conversations coming from a few of the open doorways. We walk quickly past those and are almost to the main doors leading out of the office area when Joss flashes into one of the offices, nearly causing my heart to stop. She comes back out just as fast with a sneaky smile and something clutched in her fist. I give her an annoyed look but just wave her ahead. I can find out later what she snatched.

When we get to the doors that lead out into the main barracks, she taps me on the shoulder.

"Stop being sneaky. We should walk around like we're allowed to be out here, less chance of us being questioned."

I give her a knowing nod. She's right, sneaking around will look suspicious so I straighten up and lift my head before shoving the doors open and stepping through. What we see and hear on the other side is a complete contrast to the near empty and silent office and living quarters we just came from. Here are most of the people and the noise is much louder. I don't know why but it makes me feel a little less scared. Maybe it's because I don't feel quite so alone in this crazy situation.

Joss tugs my arm to move us away from the doors and we start slowly skirting the huge cavern as we watch what's happening in the center area where all the bunks are. Men and women are making up bunks with sheets and blankets from sealed plastic bags and talking amongst themselves in small groups. There's a tension coming from them with some having worried looks and some with angry expressions but no one is yelling or demanding answers like I want to do.

We keep moving around the perimeter and pass a set of washrooms for men and women. When we reach the first corner, the rock wall changes to a double set of glass doors that automatically slide open when we pass the sensor. I quick look in shows me that it's filled with medical looking instruments and a few hospital beds. There's a soldier standing at one of the counters who looks up from his clipboard as the doors open. His mouth opens in surprise as his eyes track from me to Joss before snapping shut with a frown causing me to quicken my steps past the doors. I push Joss ahead of me expecting a hand to land on my shoulder at any moment but a quick glance behind shows me that the soldier hasn't come after us.

I stumble into Joss as she comes to a halt in front of me and I step to the side to see why she's stopped. There's a line of soldiers blocking our way ahead as they wait to be handed what looks like a stack of clothing from a storage room door. It only takes one of them to notice us before it ripples down the line and we find at least twenty pairs of eyes staring at us. I swallow down hard at the attention and reach for Joss' arm to start pulling her away when a voice barks out causing me to flinch.

"What's this, then? Where did you two come from?"

It takes me a few seconds to process the words that are directed at us in a French-Canadian accent from the soldier at the front of the line. His expression is slightly amused as he taps his clipboard giving me the courage to respond.

"Uh, we, uh…My dad, he's General Mallor," I stutter out.

The man's eyebrows pop up towards his hairline in surprise before he nods in understanding.

"Right! Ok, this is supply and my name is Major Boucher. You come to me when you need anything." He looks us up and down before yelling back into the supply room. "Captain Roy, bring me the tape!"

Joss moves closer to me and clutches my hand uncertainly as we wait for whatever the tape is under the eyes of the twenty soldiers standing in line. A younger soldier comes out with a fabric tape measure in his hand and scans the line at the door before following their eyes to where Joss and I stand. His mouth opens to speak but then he closes it, shrugs and takes a knee in front of us where he quickly measures our legs, arms, and waists while calling out the numbers to the Major. As soon as he finishes he disappears back into the supply room.

"I need your names. AIRIA will notify you when we have made some alterations to the stock we have so you'll both have a few changes in clothing."

Joss and I give him our names and he writes them down on his clipboard before waving us further down the wall.

"Next door is where you get your bathroom kit. Off you go kids!"

We both let out breaths of relief when all eyes turn away from us and he addresses the next soldier in line. We keep our heads down as we cut through the line and make our way to the next one that is just as long. This time we go to the end of it and wait our turn. I'm surprised that no one really seems to care that there are two kids in the bunker filled with adults but after studying the faces around me, I realize that they are way more worried about what's happening outside the bunker than in it.

We skip the next two lines because we don't know what they're for and make our way around the rest of the perimeter with our plastic bathroom bags clutched to our chests. We pass more washrooms and a huge section that looks like a cafeteria area before we make it back to the office doors and slide through them. There's a group of soldiers standing in the hallway talking in hushed tones right in front of us that see us right away. They all stare at us for a moment before turning and entering a set of metal doors on the left side of the hall that leads away from the offices. Joss and I move quickly to get a look into the room and see walls filled with computer screens and monitors showing the outside world. I catch my breath when I see my father standing in the middle of the room with his arms crossed as people move around him. As if he feels my presence, he starts to turn around but thankfully the doors close before he can spot us and we double-time it back to our living quarters.

As soon as we get back into our room, a grin splits across my face at a successful adventure but it disappears just as fast when the floor rocks under our feet sending me staggering to the side and Joss towards the couch. She lets out a short scream to match my own. The heaving keeps going for what feels like forever but is only actually a half a minute before it all stops. I push myself back to my feet and rush over to Joss who's pulling herself up from the couch with a pale face.

"Are you ok?" I ask her as I help steady her.

"She gives a brief nod before looking around the room and then settling her gaze on the speaker in the corner of the ceiling.

"AIRIA? What just happened?"

"Joslin Frost, local tremors have occurred from secondary bombs striking Ottawa and Montreal."

Our eyes lock onto each other's as fear washes through me.

"Are we ok?" I ask both Joss and computer.

"Jackson Mallor, bunker damage analysis is ongoing. Current analysis shows eight percent integrity reduction."

I look at Joss in confusion. "What the heck does that mean?"

She lets out a deep sigh. "That means there was some damage to the bunker but we're ok. I think."

She grabs her tablet that had fallen to the carpet, thumbs it awake and glances at the screen before carefully setting it on the coffee table in front of the couch.

"One hour, forty-six minutes since I sent the email to my parents."

I bite down on my lip before trying to reassure her.

"Then they are probably far away from the city. I bet they got together with my mom and are almost here by now."

Joss nods slowly without conviction but I don't really believe that either. We sit quietly, lost in our own thoughts on the couch for hours. We're in a holding pattern, just waiting for something to change or someone to come. After a while, my eyes droop and I slide into sleep where the world is a back to normal.

Joslin

Jackson's soft breathing tells me he has fallen asleep and I envy him. I wish I could let go and just drift away from all this madness too. I glance down at my tablet, over four hours since I sent the email. I try and picture where they might be and how they must be feeling if they actually got it. Did they get in touch with Jackson's Mom and does she know about this place? Are they as scared as I am? I sigh and clutch my tablet tighter. It's not fair. After all the time I spent without a family, all alone in this crappy world, to finally find one and start feeling loved only to have it stolen away again. I want to scream, cry and rage but that's never gotten me very far in the past so instead, I do what I've always done when I've taken a hit, I suck it all back and bury it deep inside. If I'm stuck here, then I need to try and control what I can so I stand up and go into the small bedroom with bunks and close the door quietly so I don't wake up Jackson. I pull out the items I had stolen from one of the offices earlier and study them. A set of wireless earbuds with a charging cord and three memory sticks. They aren't anything special but they might mean a lot to me in the future. At some point, my tablet will probably wear out and there's pictures, videos, and files on it that I will want to save, so the memory sticks will be my back up. The earbuds might be even more important.

Jackson's dad sees me as a tag along and a nuisance right now. I'm not important to him or anyone else in this place. I have to plan on my parents not getting here so I will need to look out for myself. The only way I'll get any information is if I can stay connected to the computer that runs this place. I'm pretty sure the General only gave me a yellow clearance so Jackson and I would be out of his hair. It would only take a few words from him to change that and then I'd be completely in the dark. I'm going to need to keep my head down and stay off his radar. Hopefully, he'll forget about me and the access I have to AIRIA. For that to happen, I need to be able to communicate with her without reminding him about it. The earbuds might be a way for that to happen.

I look up at the ceiling and speak.

"Um, AIRIA, is there a way for you to connect to these earbuds and answer me through them instead of coming through the room's speakers? I uh, don't want to wake Jackson up."

"Joslin Frost, I am capable of syncing with any wireless device to communicate with you, as well as the tablet you are holding."

I glance down at the tablet and a small smile tugs at my lips. This might work even better. If she could communicate with text instead of voice then no one would hopefully know.

"Can you use text on my tablet instead of voice? I wouldn't want to be a distraction to others nearby if I had questions for you."

"Joslin Frost, affirmative. I would utilize the messaging app on your tablet. Which method do you prefer to use, text or voice response through the earbuds?"

"Let's go with text for now. I'll let you know if I want to change to vocal in the future."

The speaker stays silent but the messaging app chimes. I tap it open to see an affirmative response to my choice of text. The battery icon shows me that I only have twenty-two percent of power left so I leave the room and find my backpack. Thankfully, I have my charging cable in there or I'd just have a paperweight instead of a tablet when the battery dies. I find the nearest power outlet and let it charge while I take the time to back up the files I want to keep. I don't let myself look at all the pictures that I've taken in the last few years. I can't let myself mourn my new family until I'm sure that they won't show up. I fill up two of the sticks with the pictures, videos, music and some of the small programs I've learned to create since I caught the coding bug leaving me with one blank stick for future use. I stare down at the pitiful amount of life and memories I've stored on two sticks and sigh. It's not much but it's all that I have and I plan on keeping it. I learned early on in life that I couldn't trust anyone but myself so I slide the memory sticks into a side pocket of my lunch bag. I doubt anyone would think to look in there if they decide to search my stuff.

Jackson's still sleeping on the couch so I spend the next hour typing questions to AIRIA in the armchair beside the couch. I don't want to be alone even if he's sleeping. I find out about the many levels in the bunker and where everything is located as well as where I can go. There are some areas that are off-limits to my clearance level but most of the place is clear if I wanted to spend the next few weeks exploring. I download and save the maps to each level knowing that they'll come in handy in the future. I've just started to comb through some of the inventory lists when the door opens making me jump.

The General stands in the doorway taking in his sleeping son with a frown on his face. When his head turns my way, I put the tablet in sleep mode and slide it between the cushion and side of the chair out of view. I keep my eyes on him and try not to shrink while he studies me. With a slight nod towards me, he turns away and finally steps into the room and strides towards the dining table. Donnelly follows behind him with two cafeteria trays stacked on top of each other. They have plates with covers on them and it only takes seconds for the smell of food to hit me. My stomach growls loudly causing my cheeks to redden in embarrassment when both of the men turn to stare at me.

Donnelly looks away quickly but the General just sighs in annoyance like my hunger is such an inconvenience to him.

"Donnelly set those down and go get another tray for Miss…" He arches an eyebrow at me, waiting for me to provide a name. I swallow the dislike I have for this man but am not surprised at all that he wouldn't remember the stray kid his son had brought with him.

"Frost, Joslin Frost."

He turns to his aide and waves him away before settling down at the table and reaching for one of the food trays. He lifts the cover revealing some type of meat, mashed potatoes and limp green beans with brown gravy covering half of it. As he goes to set the cover to one side he glances my way and his hand stops briefly before returning the cover to the plate and pushing the tray to the side. He uses his foot under the table to shove the chair across from him from out under the table and points to it with a sharp finger jab.

I keep my head down as I cross the room and settle warily into it with one quick glance back at Jackson's sleeping form. He's not going to be a buffer for me this time. The silence drags on until I can't stand it so I lift my eyes from the table to look straight at the General.

"My son seems very attached to you."

I just nod my head at this and wait.

"How long have the two of you been friends?" He asks in a neutral tone.

"Two years, sir. Jackson is my best friend."

He leans back and continues to study me before sighing. "Do you understand what's happening out there?"

Again, I just nod my head and wait.

"Then you understand that from this point forward, things will be different. I have certain expectations of my son and they don't include any of the childish nonsense that the two of you have been enjoying. Hard decisions have to be made. We are at war now and the most important thing will be survival. To that effect, Jackson will begin training to be a soldier. His time will be filled with more important things than hanging out with a girl. You will also need to be trained. We will all need to work hard to keep this place running smoothly. There's no free lunch in this new world."

When I just nod my head again, he waves his hand dismissively.

"I will have Donnelly find a suitable female instructor that will mentor you. He will find a bunk for you out in the barracks."

I murmur a "Yes, sir." as he pulls his meal tray back in front of him, removes the cover and begins to eat. I'm not sure if I should leave the table but when my stomach growls again, he glances over at Jackson and shakes his head before nudging the second tray towards me.

"You might as well eat that one. He can have the one Donnelly went to get."

I whisper, "Thank you, sir" and manage to get half the food eaten while my stomach rolls with nerves. He's going to separate Jackson and me and I will once again be alone. Just like most of my life, I won't have any allies or anyone to watch my back. I can just imagine the resentment the random woman will feel when she's stuck with a ten-year-old girl to babysit. At least the foster families I had been placed with before got paid a monthly check. This woman will have to do it for free. I can only hope whoever gets stuck with me will be halfway kind about it. My mind is swirling with the what-ifs of my future when the messenger app on my tablet gives a muffled chime from the armchair.

My whole body freezes with the fork full of potatoes halfway to my lips when the General barks. "What the hell was that?"

I swallow painfully against the dryness in my throat, set the fork back onto my plate and take a sip of water to stall for time. He's glaring around the room searching for the source of the chime when inspiration comes to me.

"I'm sorry, sir. It's just a game I was playing on my tablet. I forgot to shut it off."

His glare settles back onto me but eases after a few seconds so he must believe me.

"Well, I hope you enjoyed it because there won't be time for games after today. I expect you to train hard and learn to carry your own weight!"

I nod my head but am spared a reply when Donnelly bangs through the door with the extra food tray.

"Sir! You're needed in the command room. The computer has detected a perimeter breach!"

I can't help the gasp of hope that rushes down my throat at Donnelly's words. They made it! I won't be alone after all. It feels like a thousand-pound weight has lifted off my shoulders but the General spears me with a look. He must have assumed my gasp was one of fright because his next words sent the weight crashing back down on to me.

"You have nothing to fear. Now that there's been a strike so close to us the doors are sealed. They will not open for anyone. No one is getting in. No one!"

I feel all the blood drain from my face as he shoves away from the table and strides out of the room with Donnelly at his heals, the food tray having been dumped on the counter. I stare at the door and shake my head slowly. He wouldn't do that. He wouldn't leave Jackson's mom and my family out there to die. Would he? I flash back to all my classmates sitting in the theatre where he sent them to wait while we evacuated. He didn't care about all those kids that are now probably dead so why would he care about my family? I push away from the table and stagger over to the armchair to retrieve my tablet and see the perimeter breach message from AIRIA. My fingers start flying over the keyboard with all the questions I need answers to but it's taking too long to type it all in so I rush into the bedroom and close the door.

"AIRIA, how many people are outside right now? Is it possible to let them in? Are the doors really sealed to everyone? Is there radiation outside the doors right now?"

"Joslin Frost, eighteen people detected inside the perimeter. Your clearance level does not permit you to open any exterior doors. A higher level is required. All exits are sealed to all occupants with the exception of General Mallor. Current radiation levels are within normal parameters for human exposure. Estimated time of radiation increasing due to multiple nuclear strikes in the vicinity coupled with wind patterns is seven hours and eighteen minutes."

I lean back and blow out a breath. Ok, the General can open the doors and let them in. I was afraid that the doors would be sealed for some amount of time because of radiation, but according to AIRIA, he can open them anytime he wants. I chew on my bottom lip while going over all the different scenarios of how Jackson and I will live here with our families until my standard pessimist mood overwhelms me. I know better than to get my hopes up that things will go my way. I have no way of knowing if my parents or Jackson's mom are even in the group outside.

"AIRIA, is there any way to identify the people outside the doors right now?"

"Joslin Frost, facial recognition scans did not find any matches to current military data banks."

I rub my forehead in frustration. Her answer doesn't help me at all until I realize that to do facial recognition, the computer would need to be able to scan the faces of the people out there and that means...

"AIRIA, are there external cameras and if there is, can I see the feed on my tablet?"

"Joslin Frost, yes there are external cameras. Patching feed to your device now. Stand-by."

I hold my breath in anticipation for the few seconds it takes for a video icon to appear on my screen and try not to stab it with my finger. I bounce in place as the app loads and a four-split video appears. The top two views just show trees but the bottom two have people milling around on them so I tap the first one to turn it to full screen and hold the tablet close to my face as I try and recognize any of the people in view. There are both men and women as well as a few children on the feed with a few vehicles including an antique looking school bus parked in the background but I don't recognize any of them. I'm slightly relieved to see other kids out there so Jackson and I won't be the only young people stuck in here for the next however many years we will be forced to stay inside, but my main concern is finding my parents. I minimize the feed and open the second one. The instant it pops up, my breath catches in my throat as relief surges through me. There they are! My parents, Jackson's mom, and two other people are front and center on the screen. My relief quickly turns to confusion at the expressions on their faces. They all look angry and their mouths are moving sharply like they are yelling at someone.

A hot ball of nausea rolls in my stomach. The only reason they could be that angry is if they are not being allowed inside. Why wouldn't the General let them in? There's no danger to anyone inside at the current radiation levels so he could easily just open the door and allow our parents in. This doesn't make any sense! There's more than enough room in this place for a few more people. What the heck is going on?

I quickly tap the record icon on the video and surge to my feet. I have to show this to Jackson and get him to talk to his dad. There's no way he'd let him leave his mom out there to die. I rush to the bedroom door and jerk it open, intent on waking Jackson up but he's no longer on the couch where I left him. He standing at the entrance to the unit with a woman wearing a uniform. Her hair is pulled back into a severe bun that goes along with the scowl on her face. Jackson's expression when he turns my way is one of panicked uncertainty. He opens his mouth to speak but she beats him to it.

"Frost? Joslin Frost?"

When I just stand there frozen, her scowl deepens until I give a brief nod of my head. She lifts a hand and twirls her finger in the air.

"Grab your kit and let's go. You've been assigned to a bunk in the general barracks."

My eyes flash to Jackson's for a brief moment but I know he won't be able to stop this right now so I just turn away and start gathering up the few things I had removed from my backpack. It'll just be easier to go along with this for now. My parents will hopefully be inside soon and we will be together. With my back to the entrance, I use my body to conceal the tablet and quickly thumb it to life. The video feed shows the same thing as a few minutes ago so I mute the notifications and stuff it down into my pack with the charger just as Jackson grabs my arm.

"Joss, I'll talk to my dad when he gets back and sort this out. I won't let him separate us!"

I give him a small smile. "It's ok, Jacks. They're here. My parents and your mom are outside right now. They'll sort something out once they get inside."

His eyes flare wide with excitement and relief before turning to uncertainty.

"How do you know that?"

I glance over my shoulder at the woman and see that she's stepped closer to us so I just give a half shrug and pat his arm. I don't know if I'll be allowed to keep the yellow clearance I have with AIRIA so it's better if I keep quiet and hope they forget that I have it. Until my family gets inside, it's the only control I will have over my circumstances.

Joslin

"Let's go!" Is barked at me so I heave out a breath and turn away from my only friend. I follow the woman out the door and through the hallways until we're back in the barracks. She doesn't speak to me again but I steal quick glances at her face as we walk. Her red swollen eyes counteract her stern expression and tell me that she's just as upset to be here as I am. I turn away from her and look into every face we pass and see the same emotions on the soldiers lounging or standing around the bunks we pass. All these people are feeling the same things. Uncertainty, fear, and sadness for their friends and family members that are still out in the war-torn world.

A few of them stare at me as we walk past but most of them gaze blankly at the floor or in front of themselves with lost expressions. We reach a section of bunks that is filled with female soldiers and they take a greater interest in me than the male soldiers we had passed. Questions are tossed out to the woman I'm following but she just ignores them and keeps walking until we come to a set of empty bunks. She stabs a finger at the bottom bunk and without even looking at me, speaks.

"This is you. Go to supply and get a bedroll, make up your bunk then stay here until I tell you." That's all she says before turning on her heel and walking away.

My shoulders slump as I look around at the closest bunks but they're just as empty as the one she's assigned to me so I head over to the area where Jackson and I had gotten our bathroom kits and find the door for bedding and towels. There isn't a line this time so I'm given what I need quickly from the clerk with a check ticked on a clipboard and head back to my new bunk. I've barely managed to open the clear plastic bag protecting the sheet set when there's an incredibly loud noise from the front of the barracks that echoes through the huge room.

My head swings in every direction but all I see is women with bewildered and fearful expressions staring in the direction that the sound came from. Before the noise, there had been a quiet murmur of many people talking or moving around but now there was complete silence. I expect AIRIA or the General to make some kind of announcement to let the soldiers know what was happening but the speakers stay silent. I turn to grab my backpack and the tablet inside it to ask AIRIA what is happening when there's another huge crash from the same area followed seconds later by an even bigger roar that is clearly an explosion. There's no silence after that as people yell and scream as the lighting in the bunker changes from the harsh white of the many large halogen lights to a flashing blood red of alarms. Over all of this, AIRIA's voice finally booms out.

"Main barracks external door compromised. An analysis shows thirty-six percent integrity reduction. Recommend evacuation to lower levels within the next six hours to avoid radiation contamination."

Her voice repeats the message over and over again until it abruptly cuts off in mid-sentence leaving an echoing silence in the cavern that rapidly fills with many voices filled with fear and confusion. I stand by my bunk, frozen. Those explosions had to have been the people outside trying to get in. I can't understand any of it. Why didn't the General just let them in? Why would my family and Jackson's mom try and damage the bunker that would save all of our lives when the radiation got here? None of this makes any sense to me but mainly I'm just terrified of what will happen next to the people outside and us inside.

The sounds that come seconds later answer my fears for my parents and the ones outside. The harsh rat-tat-tat of rapid gunfire is muted through the walls of the bunker but every person inside crouches lower at the sound. Except for the muted gunfire, silence blankets the room. It seems to go on forever as I lower myself to the stone floor and let the tears flow down my cheeks. I know without ever checking the video feed that the General is killing every person outside the doors. I don't know how long I sit there on the floor before I realize the shooting has stopped and then the speakers come alive with the General's voice.

"Attention! Attention! This facility has been attacked by enemy combatants. We have neutralized the threat but they have succeeded in damaging the integrity of the main doors. We will be forced to relocate all personnel to the lower levels. This will be done in an orderly manner. There are just over six hours until the radiation from the nuclear strikes reaches this area. That is more than enough time for us to remove the majority of the supplies we will require from this level. I expect every single one of you to continue to honor your uniform and country by following command and keeping calm. Together we will survive and thrive once the threat to our country and lives are over. Orders to follow from your individual troop leaders, General Mallor out."

As the murmur of conversation picks back up all around me, I know I'm in shock because all I can think about is how steady the General's voice had been when he announced that the enemy had been neutralized. I know that's another way of saying they were all dead. He didn't even have the smallest tremor in his voice after murdering the mother of his only child and a group of innocent men, women, and children. My family is dead and we're all going to be ruled over by a monster.

End Interlude...

Chapter Two...Skylar

I clutch Ben tighter to me and stare defiantly at Uncle Bill, waiting for him to answer me. The anger is plain to see in his eyes but I don't know if it's directed at me and my accusation or at the idiot who fired his rifle at me.

He makes it pretty clear that it's me he's mad at when he roughly barks back, "Everything here is a threat until we have determined otherwise. That includes all of these people. Until we have assessed the situation and the personnel here, you will all follow every command issued. Skylar, leave the boy and come with me. There are things I need to discuss with you."

He turns on his heel and marches away expecting me to follow along like a lap dog but he doesn't know me. This dog has teeth! I turn back to my people and gently peel Ben off of me so I can kneel down in front of him.

"Hey kiddo, I know this is very scary and being outside is overwhelming but I need you to know that everything is going to be ok. I'm going to go talk to that guy and sort all of this out but for right now I need you to stay with Belle and Matty and do whatever these soldiers say. Can you do that for me?"

His lower lip quivers but he gives me a brave little nod. I'm about to stand and leave him when his small hand clutches me tighter.

"Sky, can you find AIRIA? I'm scared without her."

I have to bite hard on my tongue to keep the tears from welling up in my eyes because I want so bad to cry, "me too!" AIRIA might just be a computer program made up of ones and zeros but to me and especially to Ben, she's our parent. Instead, I suck it deep down and let anger fill me. I give him a nod and a kiss and then hand him off to Belle. As I turn to leave, I make eye contact with Rex, Marsh, Ethan, Lance and all the others one by one. They're all looking to me to fix this. It's ironic that not too long ago I was willing to leave them all out here to the mercy of the snow and ash but now I will fight for their lives like they were my own. I try and give a reassuring nod to them but I'm afraid it will just come off as scared so I quickly turn away.

I've only got a few steps in the direction that Uncle Bill went when I see another, older soldier striding towards me with a thunderous expression on his face.

"The General gave you an order, young lady!" He snarls as he reaches out a hand to grab me.

I jerk back out of reach and snarl right back, "Touch me and I'll put you in the dirt!"

He rears back in surprise but then smirks with condescension for a second before freezing at what I say next.

"Try me. Go ahead and see your men laugh when little girl me drops you in under twenty seconds…try…me." It's said with a flat, cold tone, low so only he hears. He must have seen something in my eyes to convince him because he lets his hand drop and jerks his head in the direction I was going anyways. I step around him and don't bother even looking at him again. The door leading into the airlock of mine and Ben's quarters is standing open so I head that way, assuming that is where Uncle Bill has gone.

As the door slides closed, I try and tamp down the rage that's filled me. This guy has the upper hand right now and blasting him the way I want to won't get me very far. I need to try and stay calm and reasonable to make this work. That turns into an even bigger challenge for me when the door slides open in front of me and I see him helping himself to food from my fridge. I bite down on the nasty words that fill my mouth and want to spew out and instead, take a seat at the kitchen island with a blank expression.

He nods at me as he continues to assemble the sandwich he's making on the counter. He holds up a ripe red tomato in one hand and stares at it before pinning me with his ice blue eyes.

"You have no idea how lucky you've been for the last seven years."

I don't bother answering him even though he's wrong on that count. I know the food part has been lucky for Ben and me but there's so much more than just fresh food to being lucky. We've faced our own devastating losses that no amount of fresh produce can make up for. I keep quiet and wait for what he has to say next.

He starts speaking as he slices up the tomato.

"I understand that this will be a huge adjustment for you but your father and I had a plan for all of this to happen. My people will take their rightful place in the main barracks as it was built for them. We will set up the tents outside for all the others you allowed in and continue to feed them and provide security. Within the next few days, we will begin locating suitable farmland to plow under and start planting with the equipment and supplies that we stocked this place with. Your people and other survivors that we have gathered on the journey here from the east will help with the labor. Rebuilding this world will take each and every person working towards it."

I think about his words and how they align with our own plans as he begins eating. They sound exactly like what we had wanted to do but his tone puts me off so I ask, "Will we be working with you or for you? What of the people who want to go their own way and do their own thing?"

He takes his time chewing and swallowing before answering me.

"Skylar, we can do this the easy way or the hard way. This isn't a democracy anymore. Every person here will answer to me and follow my orders, including you."

There's no emotion in his words, just a statement of fact. "So, what you're saying is, we're your prisoners? Your slave laborers and we have no say over anything in our lives?"

He lifts one shoulder in a shrug. "If that's how you want to spin it, then yes. I plan on rebuilding and I'm fine with however that is accomplished. As I said, we will feed, house and secure the people out there but they will earn it by doing the work that needs to be done."

I grit my teeth as I ask my final question. "And Ben and me? Where do we fit in? Will we be relocated out to one of the tents as well? Are we to lose our home now that you're here?"

His eyes narrow at my tone and then glance around the room, taking in all the comforts we've had since the bombs dropped before coming back to me.

"Yes, this was your home but I think it's important for you to get the right mindset right off the bat. This place was on loan to your father. He was a caretaker, nothing more. You've grown accustomed to being in charge here and that will be hard to give up. I think it's best if you and your brother join the rest of the people outside in the tents to better come to terms with your new place in the world."

Cold, hard hate for this man fills every bit of my being. First, he takes AIRIA from us and now he's taking our home too. If I had a weapon on me I wouldn't hesitate to end this man's existence. He's no family of mine and I doubt he was ever a true friend to my father. I've lost everything so I no longer have to be reasonable and I let my real feelings show with a heavy dose of sarcasm.

"Well, thank goodness that of all the people to survive the bombs, it was my godfather! Can you imagine how awful it would have been if it was an enemy who showed up and took everything from me?"

His eyes are cold and his chuckle lacks any actual humor when he shakes his head at me.

"Oh Skylar, I'm not your enemy and you haven't lost everything…yet. There is so much more you could lose if you cross me."

I suck in a breath of shock. There's only one thing I have left to lose and he's waiting for me outside. I don't know why I'm surprised that this man would threaten the life of a child but it makes it very clear that he is my enemy and that means…war.

I hear the door slide open behind me and turn away from him to see his son and the girl I had ridden here with come in. Jackson is looking uncertainly between his father and me but the girl looks around my home with something like recognition on her face. Like she's just come home after being away for a long time. It creeps me out so I turn back to the man who once upon a time was my uncle but now is just the General.

"Am I allowed to take a few belongings from here for Ben and me? I'm sure you wouldn't want to have to look at the faces of your dear friends, my parents, in all these pictures. That would be…awkward, wouldn't it?"

He smirks at me and waves his half-eaten sandwich towards the bedrooms.

"One bag for each of you is fine." He turns to his son. "Jackson, go with her. Make sure she doesn't pack any weapons."

I turn from him in disgust and see the disbelief on his son's face as I walk past him to a closet to grab two of the bug out bags that have been packed for years.

"Dad, you can't be serious! You can't just kick them out of here. It's their home!" I hear Jackson say in an outraged voice. I don't hear whatever his dad says in response as I go into Ben's room to grab a few changes of clothes and some of his small treasures. I catch sight of the girl standing in the doorway from the corner of my eye but ignore her as I fill the pack until it bulges.

"I'm Joslin." She says in a low voice.

I don't care who she is or what her name is so I don't respond. I hear her sigh as I struggle to close the clasp on the overfilled pack and catch the motion of her walking into the room. Once the clasp closes, I heft the bag on to my shoulder and turn to leave for my room but she's blocking my way and in her hands is a very special toy. She holds it out to me.

"He'd want this, don't you think?"

My blood goes cold as I stare hard at her. Who the frack is this girl and how does she know anything about me or Ben and that Quackers the duck is his version of a security blanket? I snatch it out of her hands.

Who are you?"

She glances over her shoulder into the main room before looking back at me with pleading eyes.

"A friend. One you can trust. I…you need to trust me. I will fix this!" She says in a whisper.

Trust? I can count the people I trust on one hand and whoever this girl is, she's not one of them. I give her a small shake of my head and brush past her, dumping the pack on the floor beside the couch and grabbing the next one for my stuff. I mindlessly pull clothes out of drawers and pictures from frames until this pack is bulging too. I'd love to take more but I can't sacrifice the survival gear for mementos of a former life.

I leave my room without a second glance for fear of my emotions getting the best of me and add the second bag to the other one on the floor before looking around our main living space. My mother's art on the walls, the wooden carvings my father had made to fill the space would all be left here. I have to be practical with the things I take from here…for now. This will not be the last time I'm in my home. I don't know how but I'll find a way to get back all that these people are taking from me! I take a quick look over to the General and his son who are both watching me. Jackson just looks sad and embarrassed but the General mocks me by raising a glass of milk to me before taking a big gulp. I want to smash that glass into his face and the urge makes me reckless so I march over to the closet and grab another bag, this one empty, before slipping into the bathroom and cleaning the counters of all our bathroom gear. I stuff it with all the extra toothbrushes and paste plus soap, deodorant, and shampoo that I had stored under the counter before marching back out and into the kitchen where I glare defiantly at the General.

"This might be your bunker but I grew that food and milked that cow and I'm taking some of it out there with me!" I wait for a negative reaction from him but instead his expression turns to amusement.

"Be my guest but I'm not sure how much space you have left in your TWO bags."

I bark right back at him, "I'm taking THREE!"

His eyebrows shoot up in mocking surprise before lowering into a scowl but Jackson interrupts before he can deny me.

"Dad! Come on!" He pleads on my behalf.

The General doesn't acknowledge his son's words but his scowl lessens as he takes another gulp of milk before answering.

"You know what? That meal was so satisfying that I'm feeling generous. You go ahead and take that third bag, honey. Consider it payment for taking care of my property all these years."

His words are so thick with condescension that they practically drip with it. I want nothing more than to lunge over to the knife on the counter he had used to cut the tomato and plunge it into his stomach but I just turn away instead and go to work gathering as much food from the fridge and pantry that I can fit in the bag. Once it's full, I ignore everyone in the room and throw it on my back before gathering the other two bags and stomp to the airlock door. I open my mouth to ask AIRIA to open it when it hits me again that she won't respond to anything I have to say so I just stand there, too proud to ask him to open the door for me.

I hear him chuckle behind me and feel a wash of defeat flow through me. All the anger, rage, and vengeance I felt is slowly draining away and being replaced by sheer exhaustion from the long day and all-nighter I'd had trying to rescue Rex and Sasha, plus the events of today. I just want out of here. I want to be with my family and my friends. I'm almost grateful when the girl, Joslin, addresses AIRIA and the door slides open in front of me. As I walk out, I know at some point in the future I will be back but for now, I've lost the battle.

Chapter Three...Rex

Matty throws himself against me in relief as I watch Skylar disappear into the airlock. Things played out so fast down at the hotel that I didn't even get to speak to her before we were separated and shoved into the troop transporter. I hold Matty tight against me and look around at my small group within the larger group that's lined up out here. Belle is sobbing softly into Sasha's hair in relief to have her back while keeping a firm grip on Ben whose eyes stay locked on the airlock door that his sister just disappeared through. Ethan is gently probing at the gash on Marsh's face and Lance is standing stock still with just his eyes scanning the soldiers that surround us. Matty's rambling on and on against my stomach so that I only catch every few words but the gist of it is about them being rounded up inside and forced outside. I give him a squeeze to let him know he's safe and turn away from the door to look at all the soldiers that are guarding us. They seem to be slightly more relaxed after the incident with the soldier shooting at Skylar. Maybe now that the guy in charge is here they'll dial it back a bit. At least none of them have said or done anything about us getting up off of our knees and talking to one another. Or maybe Skylar screaming at them, that they're monsters, reminded them that we're just people trying to survive too.

I look past them as even more soldiers work to unroll chain link fencing and others work at erecting huge canvas tents. I don't really know what's going on here but I can guess that we won't be enjoying the comforts of the bunker any longer. I move Matty and me closer to Lance under the harsh gaze of the guards.

"What do you think is happening, Lance?" I ask quietly.

He looks briefly down at Matty and gives a small shake of his head so I ruffle Matty's hair before steering him towards Ben, Belle, and Sasha so we can talk without him hearing.

"Hey, buddy? Can you go hang out with Ben, please? He's having a hard time being outside for the first time in his life. He could really use his friend until Sky comes back for him."

Matty gives me a small nod but not before looking at the closest soldiers in uncertainty. I grind my teeth in frustration that these guys have been so heavy handed with him that he's afraid to even move a few feet away from me. As soon as he's joined the others and distracted, I raise my eyebrows at Lance in question. His expression is grim when he answers my question.

"I would say that Skylar's godfather has come to take back what he built. Based on what I've seen since we got here, it doesn't look like he plans on sharing it with us."

I take another look over at the airlock and see the two teens that had been in Skylar's Hummer go in but there's no sign of Skylar coming out. She's been through so much since I met her and Ben and even worse before that. She's finally opened herself to sharing her world and home with other people but now it's all shifted on her again. I wince when I remember the anguish in her voice back at the hotel when AIRIA wouldn't respond to her and the look of complete loss on her face when the man had told that AIRIA was no longer hers. I don't know how she's going to deal with that.

I blow out a breath of concern for her and ask Lance, "What about Sky? This guy was her family, right? He'll take care of her and Ben, won't he?"

Lance lifts one shoulder in a shrug but his eyes never stop moving over the soldiers when he answers.

"Not by blood. This Bill guy was just a family friend. She said he and her Dad served together. I'm not sure how much weight that will carry after all this time. Especially as the world sits right now." He glances over at Ethan, Marsh and the others before continuing. "For now, we wait and see what their plans are but we might have to get out of here fast, depending on what they have planned for us, so be ready to go at a moment's notice."

I nod in understanding before moving over to join the others and settle down beside Marsh on the dead grass. He's holding what looks like a ripped portion of a shirt against the gash on his head. We lost our packs when the soldiers took us into custody so Ethan doesn't have any medical supplies to properly bandage the wound Marsh got at the hotel. It's held together with a few butterfly bandages but blood is still weeping from it. I bump shoulders with him and shoot him a grin.

"Hey man, I never got the chance to thank you for coming to the rescue. Those psychos were going to have us for their main dinner course!"

Marsh screws up his face in disgust and then winces as the movement pulls at his wound.

"Dude! Do you think they'd have put you in the soup or Hannibal Lecter'd you with fava beans?"

A cold shiver runs down my spine even as I laugh at his words. I'm glad Sasha and I made it out of that horror show.

I shake the feeling away and ask, "How's the head?"

He smirks. "Just a scratch, man. Just a scratch." He waves a hand at the men guarding us. "Any idea what's up with the G.I. Joes? You think they're here to save the day or be our overlords?"

I shake my head and shrug. I know as much as he does. All we can do is wait for someone to tell us what comes next. Ben and Matty get tired of standing and come sit with us. They're both way quieter than normal as they lean against Marsh and me for comfort. We all sit and wait while we watch the huge tents going up and fences being erected around the clearing but my eyes keep going back to the airlock. I think back to the last time I really talked to Sky. We were getting ready for the Thanksgiving party and she had a sparkle in her eye. We were laughing about having our first party with music and how neither of us even knew how to dance. The last time I saw her before the brief moment at the hotel was when she went with the girls over to her quarters to get ready for the party. She was so excited and happy. It makes me so sad to realize that it was the first time I had ever really seen her happy. It feels like so long ago, but it was less than twenty-four hours ago and now everything's changed again.

The airlock door slides to the side and I jolt to my feet when I see Skylar stumble out under the weight of three backpacks. Her expression is the complete opposite of the one she wore when she stomped furiously in there. Her shoulders are slumped from more than the weight of the bags. She looks completely defeated and without hope. I want to rush over to her and help her with the bags but there's a line of soldiers between us and even if they have relaxed a little, I think they'd see me rushing at them as a threat so I'm forced to just wait.

When she reaches the line of men, she barely looks up from the ground and her voice is low when she says, "Move". The two men closest to her look over their shoulders at her and then slide apart until she passes them. Once she's on my side of the line, I move towards her and relieve her of two of the bags. Her lips barely move in the briefest of smiles but her eyes stay down.

"Sky!" Ben calls to her and pushes to his feet. She angles in his direction and drops the last bag from her back between them before following it down. She pulls her little brother into her lap and rests her head on his with her eyes closed. Everything about Sky screams of exhaustion. I look at the others and see that they are just as concerned about her state as I am before lowering myself down beside her and placing a hand gently on her back.

Sky? What happened inside? Are you ok?" I ask.

Her head lifts from Ben's and she turns broken eyes my way.

"He's taking over everything. He's going to start rebuilding and we will be the slaves that do it for him."

I lean back in surprise at her words and shoot a quick look at the others before asking her, "You mean, we're his prisoners?"

She nods her head but the broken expression slowly clears from her eyes, replaced by something else, something strong and she says, "Frack that!"

Chapter Four...Skylar

I sit with Ben and Rex as the others ask question after question that I can't answer. I don't have a plan and I don't know what we're going to do...yet. The only thing I know is I won't be a slave and I sure as hell won't allow Benny to be one. It's too soon for me to know how I'm going to do it. I need more information so I can see all of the angles before I can come up with a plan. Thankfully, it doesn't take long before the General comes out and tells us what he has planned for us. He strides through the ranks of his men and stops at the line. All the while looking us over like we are animals in a zoo before addressing us.

"Attention! My name is General William Mallor and I'm the highest-ranking member of the military to survive the bombings of seven years ago. The bunker you have been trespassing in belongs to me. I had it commissioned, built and stocked many years ago for an event just like the one that befell our country." He starts walking up and down the line of soldiers while addressing us. "The time has come for my men and me to take possession of the bunker and all it holds for the purpose of rebuilding. The skies have cleared and each and every one of us has a duty to commence rebuilding what we have all lost. We will begin by locating suitable farmland that we will clear of the radiated topsoil so that we may plant crops. We have already begun this clearing of the land on the journey here by doing controlled burns. We have also gathered other survivors on the way that you will join to provide the much-needed manpower to achieve all that needs to be done."

He finally stops his pacing and faces us. "We will provide you all with food, shelter, and security in exchange for your labor. As you can see, there are large troop tents going up that you will be housed in."

When he pauses for breath, a voice behind me rings out that I recognize as Lance's.

"What if we don't wish to stay here?"

A cold hard expression covers the General's face. "I'm afraid I must insist that you all remain here. It's incredibly dangerous and lawless out there and we must preserve every life that we can to help rebuild not only the infrastructure we need to thrive but also the decimated population."

I stiffened at that last part. He could only mean one thing by rebuilding the population and that means babies…lots of babies. I glance over at Belle and see she's come to the same conclusion as I have because her face is deathly pale and she clutches Sasha tight against her. I swing my eyes back to the General and see the girl, Joslin standing behind the line of soldiers. Her gaze is on the General and I've never seen such hatred directed at anyone before. She must sense me looking at her because she glances my way and the hatred in her eyes clears and is replaced by determination. Her slow nod my way just confuses me but I'm starting to think this girl might not be my enemy after all. I tuck it away for later and look back to the General who has started to speak again.

"We will relocate you to your new homes shortly and begin a census to determine your skills and abilities to better place you in your future duties. Time is of the essence as we don't know how long a growing season we will have before winter sets back in, therefore everyone will work, including women and children. There will be no free ride if we hope to accomplish as much as possible before the weather changes again." He studies us for another minute with his cold stare before barking out, "As you were!" and turns and strides away. He snaps his fingers at Joslin as he passes and with a last glance my way she follows him back to the airlock.

I turn my back on the soldiers and face my friends.

"Well, there you have it. Dear old Uncle Bill plans to use us as slave labor for crops and babies! I don't plan on doing any farming unless it's for all of us and I'm certainly not going to start having babies at the ripe old age of seventeen!"

I look every one of them in the face and see a mix of anger, fear, and confusion. I never thought I would say these words and it hurts my heart, but my choices are few.

"We have to leave. They outnumber us in personnel and weapons and I no longer have any access to AIRIA so I can't fight them. You guys can decide for yourselves but Benny and I are getting out of here as soon as possible."

Lance, Ethan, and the boys are nodding their heads but Sasha speaks up first in a defeated voice.

"There's nothing out there but death. There's nowhere to go and nothing to survive on. At least here there's food and security."

Belle pulls her daughter closer with a frown before looking to Lance for answers. He takes his time, scanning the soldiers around us before squatting down.

"We managed for seven years out there. Yes, it was hard but we lived through it. We can do it again. We'll need to think hard on where we're going, though. It will have to be far enough away from here that the soldiers won't scoop us right back up and bring us back. We need to remember as much as we can from the maps we studied when we started planning out where we were going to farm. It needs to be somewhere we can find shelter and be secure. We also have to consider the distance we want to put between us and them. We'll be on foot and probably traveling overland - making it hard to carry the supplies we'll need to get started."

Belle looks confused and asks, "What supplies? We have nothing out here and I doubt they'll give us access to anything from inside. And how are we going to secure a new place when we have no weapons? We'd be sitting ducks out there!"

Lance shakes his head and gives her a reassuring smile. "We do have resources. There are three caches around town that the boys and I set up before we moved to the hotel. There's food, water, and one of them has a rifle and small amount of ammunition in it. The supplies won't last us more than a few weeks but it will go a long way to keeping us alive while we search for a new home and scavenge for more supplies. The rifle will help us hunt and provide limited security. But, it will be a lot to carry."

Belle looks relieved but still hesitant so I lean forward to get their attention.

"I need you all to agree that this stays with us. I'm willing to add to your caches but only if it's just us. I don't really know any of the other people well enough to trust that they wouldn't sell us out and we don't have enough food to feed any more than this small group. Can we agree that this plan is for the nine of us and no one else?"

The adults all nod in agreement with Ben and Matty looking on with uncertainty. Sasha is the only one who doesn't react and with our history, I can't take a chance on her so I lean back and pin her with a hard look and grind out her name. "SASHA?"

She can't hold my gaze and drops her eyes to her lap.

"I don't want to go back out there. You don't understand what those animals that took us were going to do to us! It's safer to stay here with the soldiers to protect us."

I heave out a breath in frustration. I get that she's scared but I'm not going to give this girl a chance to sell me and Ben out again. I try one more time to get through to her.

"Sasha, do you understand that you will most likely not have any say in who your baby daddy will be? They will use you against your will until you get pregnant and once you have the baby, they'll do it again and again and again. Is that the life you're choosing?"

Belle's face morphs into one of outrage as Sasha crumples against her sobbing. "SKYLAR! Stop! There's no need for you to…"

I don't let her finish.

"There's EVERY need to, Belle! Your daughter is the weak link in this. She's already sold me and my brother out once and her recklessness yesterday caused a crisis that could have killed all of us." I turn away from her and send a hard look Lance's way. "I'm out. I can't take the chance of her spilling the plan to them for a better life here. I'm sorry but Ben and I will go our own way."

Everyone starts talking at once but I ignore them all and turn to Ben who has tears in his eyes as he clutches his buddy, Matty. I set a hand on his back but he shrugs it off. I sigh but say nothing. I won't let his anger stop me from doing what I need to do to keep him alive and I can't risk the few cards I have up my sleeve to betrayal.

Lances voice finally silences the rest of them with its harsh tone.

"That's ENOUGH! Keep your voices down or we won't be going anywhere. In case none of you have noticed, our captors are only ten feet away from us so pipe down and keep it to one at a time."

He glares at every one of them except me, Matty and Ben until they all look away and then continues.

"Belle, for right now I think it would be best if you took Sasha and sat away from us." He holds up a hand to silence her protests. "I promise you, we will discuss our plans with you once we have something worked out. Right now, you need to talk over some things with your daughter and really think about what you want to do and where you want to go from here."

She looks deep into his eyes and whatever she sees there convinces her to go along with him for now. Belle stands and pulls Sasha to her feet. I watch them move to a spot behind some of the other people from inside and sit back down before turning to Lance with a neutral expression. I'm willing to hear him out but I *will* do what's best for Ben and me, with or without them.

He scrubs at his face in exhaustion, reminding me that none of us have slept in over twenty-four hours and during that time we were under extreme stress. None of us are at our best and now might not be the time to make major decisions. When Ethan places a hand on Lance's back in support, he straightens back up and his face clears.

"Ok, Skylar, I also share your concerns over Sasha's state of mind so let me just say that Ethan and I will do everything possible to make sure she doesn't compromise us in any way. If for some reason Belle decides to stay here…well, it will break our hearts but it won't change our decision to leave. When it comes right down to it, we all need to do what's best for our own families and that doesn't include being a slave in my books. I know I speak for Ethan and Marsh when I say we want you and Ben with us and I know you know how Rex and Matty feel. It makes more sense for all of us to stay together. We all have different skills that we bring to the table that we will need to survive. Please, join us?"

I look down at Ben and see the pleading in his eyes. He's lost so much today that tearing him away from these people would destroy him. I also know just how hard it would be for me out there all alone trying to protect Ben and build some kind of life for us. I glance over at Rex and see the hope in his eyes before turning back to Lance and nodding my head in agreement.

"The truck is still on the service road where we hid it. In the back, there's four go bags and each one has food, water, survival gear but more importantly, each one has a handgun and a box of ammunition." I nudge two of the bags I had brought out with me. "These two have the same. The last bag is filled with food, med kits, and bathroom supplies. They never even checked them for weapons! That gives us six handguns, a rifle, and transportation. With your supply caches and my seven bags that gives us a pretty good start. As long as they don't stumble onto the truck between now and when we escape we should be able to put a fair amount of distance between us and them."

Lance reaches out and clasps my shoulder, giving it a squeeze. "Well done, Sky. Well done." He leans back and looks to the others. "Now all we need is a place to go and the opportunity to get away. I think we need to give this a few days for the dust to settle and for all of us to get some rest. For now, everyone keep your eyes open and watch. We'll find our opening, we just have to wait for it."

Everyone is nodding in agreement but Marsh looks over his shoulder at where Belle and Sasha are sitting and then heaves out a breath. "What are we going to do about them? Belle's been like a mother to us and Sasha a sister. I can't even stand the thought of what they'll be subjected to here if we leave them!"

I can tell how troubled he is by the lack of goofy surfer vocabulary. I don't want them to stay here either but Sasha makes me beyond nervous when it comes to trust. I had forgiven her for her betrayal and we had been on track to actually be friends but she's proving that every time things get hard, she can't be counted on. Lance looks over towards the girls and shakes his head.

"We won't be leaving them. Sasha's still dealing with what happened today or yesterday now, I guess. Looks like the sun's coming up. We need to let her get some sleep and calm down before we talk to her about it again. I promise her and Belle will be on board once we let them have a little time to process this. For now, we keep our plans close to our chest and leave it as need to know." He turns to me. "Skylar, I know you have misgivings based on Sasha's history but this will impact all of us if she turns on us so you have my guarantee that we will keep her under control."

Rex reaches out and takes my hand with a nod of encouragement. I don't really have a choice but to go along with it because I don't think I can keep Ben safe out here on my own.

Chapter Five...Rex

I shift the heavy weight of a sleeping Matty on my lap to try and find a more comfortable spot. He's gotten so big that he really doesn't fit in my lap anymore but I'm willing to suffer his weight to give him a few moments of peace and security. The last few months have been one upheaval and crisis after another for him and I worry about how it's affecting him. First, it was the move from the house to the hotel where we had to deal with the drama of Ted and his men, then being kidnapped and tied to a tree and left for dead. He met his first friend and got to live in the comfort of the bunker only to now have it snatched away. All these ups and downs have to be hard on a kid. All I really want for him is a stable life where he can grow and be safe. These soldiers are just one more threat to that dream.

I can't help the soft smile that crosses my face as I watch Skylar holding onto Ben. He has an amazed wonder in his expression as he sees his first sunrise. There's going to be a lot of new firsts in this kid's life as we explore a world outside of his bunker. I can't help but feel a little bit of wonder myself. There hasn't been a whole lot of sun in my world for the last seven years and to feel its soft rays on my face is sort of like a dream.

I'm distracted by the beautiful view when a group of soldiers cross the line and order some of the people to their feet. I watch about twenty of them follow along with their shoulders slumped and their heads down to one of the huge canvas tents that have been set up. There are two tables that are manned by soldiers with clipboards and from a distance, it looks like they're asking each person questions before handing them a bundle of shrink-wrapped blankets or clothing and then directing them further into the tent. I guess we're going to be assigned our new bunks. I look over and catch Belle's eye and wave her towards us with Sasha so that we can be grouped together. Just because I'm frustrated with Sasha right now doesn't mean that they're not part of my family and that I don't want them with us. I wish we had more information to go on for a plan but there's too much to consider at this point and all I really want is to fall into a bed and sleep for the next eight hours. Judging by everyone else's faces they feel the exact same way as I do.

When we are set to be the next group to be moved. Lance gathers us around him.

"Let me do the talking for us. No one say anything about Ethan and I being former military. It's best if we don't give them any reason to see us as a threat. We'll just be a family trying to survive together. Belle and Sasha, you two will be my sister and niece and Rex and Matty along with Marsh will be our sons. I'm hoping they won't separate us if we register as a single family. Skylar, they already know you and Ben aren't related to us but let's try and keep as close as possible."

Everyone gets to their feet as the guards head our way. Marsh and I help Sky with her bags as we follow the guards over to the tents without a word. We line up behind Lance and Ethan but I lean to the side to try and get a look at the guy doing the interviews. He's just a guy with a bored expression in a uniform. Nothing about him screams, "I'm your new overlord." Other than that one guy taking a warning shot at Skylar, they haven't been overly abusive or cruel. Maybe they're just people like us, trying to survive the best way they know how. Maybe the guy they're following is their best bet and even though they might not like his plans, it's all they have. Either way, their plans and our plans don't mesh. We were just starting to make our own plans to rebuild, like them, but we were going to do it as a community - not as slave labor. I'd like to give them the benefit of the doubt because I'm just flat out tired of fighting but that whole rebuilding the population thing sounds creepy and sours any chance of it.

As I wait for Lance and Ethan to answer the soldier's questions, the second table opens up, and the man sitting there with a clipboard, barks in our direction.

"Hey, some of you get in line over here!"

When none of us makes a move to go to his table he slams his clipboard down with a snap and pushes to his feet with a glare. He opens his mouth to bark at us again but Marsh preempts him.

"Chill, dude! We're all one family and your buddy's taking our deets."

The soldier scans our group and shakes his head. "B.S. There's no way this many people in one family survived!"

Skylar moves out of the line with Ben and holds up her hand to stop whatever smart-ass remark Marsh is about to impart with a weary shake of her head.

"Its fine, Ben and I can give him what he needs. Anything to get into a bed faster."

I move up closer to hear what he's going to ask but burn at the satisfied smirk that crosses his face when he asks, "Names?"

"Skylar and Ben Ross."

"Ages?"

"Seventeen and seven."

"And what skills would you say you have, Skylar Ross?"

She stares at him impassively before slowly shaking her head and then points at the doors to the bunker.

"Ask AIRIA."

He looks up at her incredulously with his pen hovering over the clipboard. "Excuse me? What would you know about AIRIA?"

I see her shoulders tighten up.

"AIRIA has basically been my Mother, Father, teacher and best friend for the last seven years. That's my home right there that you all are moving into!" She stabs a finger towards the bunker. "So, if you get anything freshly grown to eat or drink, you can thank me because I grew it, harvested it or milked it. If you want to know anything else about me or my home, ask AIRIA! Now give us a bed!"

The soldier just sits there unsure of what to say or do for a few seconds until a voice comes from behind us.

"Hey Benson, I got this one. Why don't you head inside and hand in your paperwork?"

Both Skylar, Ben and I turn around to see the teenager who was in her Hummer standing behind us. He tries to give us a smile but it's uncertain and comes off more like a grimace. It almost seems like he can't stand to hold Skylar's gaze so when she turns her back to him he flushes red and turns to me, holding out his hand.

"Hi, I'm Jackson Mallor. I'm sorry for the way this has all gone down. I didn't think it would happen this way."

I stare at his hand for a beat and decide that this might be a possible opportunity to make an ally, so I reach out my own.

"Rex Larson. I'd say it's nice to meet you but the jury's still out on that." I say with a slight grin.

He nods slowly with a chagrined expression. "Yeah, I get that. Our group has been under a lot of stress with the long journey here across the country but I'm working on my dad to ease off as best as I can. I'm hoping that once everything gets set up and organized, things will improve…for everyone."

I make a noncommittal noise and nod but before I can respond, there are three "whoosh" noises one after another above my head causing all of us to flinch and half duck.

Everyone's eyes shoot to the skies as we watch three small aircraft climb into the new blue sky.

"What the frack was that?" Skylar asks in an incredulous voice.

Jackson turns to her and says reassuringly, "It's ok! Those are drones. We're using them to search out suitable farmland and to provide overwatch security. They're no danger to us."

Skylar lets out a groan of frustration and mumbles sarcastically, "Thanks for the heads up AIRIA! Those would have come in handy during the last few weeks!"

She meets my eyes and I see the exact moment she realizes that those drones erase almost all of our option for escape. He frustration turns to anger and she swings her eyes over to Jackson.

"Can we get that bed now? We haven't slept in over twenty-four hours!" She snaps at him.

He starts nodding his head quickly. "Yes, of course! I'll get it straightened out right away!"

I feel a little bad for the guy in the face of Sky's contempt when he clearly just wants to help and make up for what his dad is doing. Once we have a bit of privacy, I'll have to talk Skylar down from her hate enough to play nice, even if it's only an act. We are running out of options fast and this guy might be our only hope if we can get him to help us.

Chapter Six...Skylar

I can hear people moving around and the low murmur of conversation near where I lay but the warm, heavy, weight of Ben pressed up against me is so comforting that I just don't want to open my eyes to join them. Instead, I think back over the ups and downs of the last few days. I'm upset by everything that's happened but I don't feel the same blind panic that I did back when Rex and Matty first entered our lives. I guess that means I'm healing, growing up or just too tired to care. I mean, somewhere in the back of my mind I knew that someday things would change. Ben and I weren't going to be all alone in the bunker for the rest of our lives, I just thought when we left it would be on our own terms. Being forced out like this after the hope I was starting to feel from the plans we had made to get started rebuilding and the party we had planned just makes me mad, furious even. Not to mention the nasty cannibals that almost took out Rex and Sasha. All I want right now is to get back into my home and chill with Ben and our old routine. Knowing that will probably never happen just makes me fracking pissed. With a deep sigh, I open my eyes.

The first thing I see is Rex staring back at me from a cot about two feet away. Like me, he has his little brother snuggled up against him on the small bed. He gives me a soft smile and says the most unexpected thing.

"I think your hair looks very pretty like that."

I reach a hand up and touch my hair in confusion and feel the satin slipperiness of the yellow ribbons that Belle had added to the waves she had created in my hair for the party. I can't believe it was only...a day or two days ago? It feels like a lifetime has passed since we were getting ready for the party.

"I'm sorry I didn't get to see you in your dress. I would have like to have a dance with you." Rex says.

I return his smile with a sad one of my own.

"Yeah, that would have been nice. I don't think there will be any dancing in our future now."

His lips tug upwards in a half smile. "You never know. Things seem to change on a dime these days."

I shake my head and say one word.

"Drones."

His expression goes grim and he lifts his head to scan around our area of the tent to make sure no one is listening to us before he answers.

"We need allies, on the inside. That guy Jackson? He seems to feel bad about how this went down. We need to use that any way we can. He was in here an hour ago with the girl with the black curls but they left when they saw most of us were still sleeping. Those two might be our way in."

"Joslin. Her name is Joslin and she has a real hate on for Jackson's dad. We definitely need to feel those two out. See where they stand on the set up here."

I shift Ben off of my arm that has gone to sleep with his weight on it and sit up to look around. All the cots surrounding us are filled with our people but I still keep my voice down.

"Have any of the soldiers come in with instructions? What are we supposed to do now and do you have any idea what time it is?"

Before Rex has a chance to answer, light floods into the tent when the flaps on the front are dragged open. I can now see that one of the tables that had been outside to check us in has been placed at the front of the tent and soldier are carrying in boxes filled with what looks like MRE's and cases of bottled water. The guy in charge of this delivery stands between us and the table with a clipboard. These guys LOVE their clipboards! He scans the people laying or sitting on cots before clearing his throat.

"ATTENTION! These are your dinner rations. One per person! If you have to use the latrines, form up in two lines by gender and you will be escorted two at a time. Otherwise, everyone must remain in the tent barracks until otherwise told. Work duties will be assigned in the morning. Lights out in two hours. That is all!"

He turns on his heel and exits the tent without another word so I slide off the cot, reposition Benny then move quickly to the front to try and get a glimpse of what's going on outside. When I reach the table, the last soldier comes through the flap with a box of MRE's. When he makes eye contact with me, I recognize him as the guy who tried to get my information earlier. When he looks away quickly, I decide to poke him a bit.

In the sweetest tone I can muster I say, "And how was YOUR dinner tonight, soldier?"

I see the red flush race up his neck into his cheeks but I'm surprised when his eyes meet mine almost defiantly.

"Actually, it was the best damn food I've eaten in the past seven years."

I glance down into the box of what I'm sure will be cardboard tasting food and then back up to his eyes with a slow nod.

"Glad you liked it. You're welcome." My voice is flat, without sarcasm. I don't know what he's gone through in the last seven years and antagonizing him won't make our situation any better but it doesn't hurt to remind him that he's eating my food. I grab two of the meals and two bottles of water and turn to go back to our cot but not before I hear him say under his breath, "Thank you." He doesn't see the tiny smile on my face. It's a start.

Dinner is a quick affair and a trip to the latrines doesn't give me any information that I can use except wondering where there were porta-potties stored in the bunker. I had never seen them in all my exploring but I also had no idea that AIRIA had drones either. The worst part of living with an AI is that you have to ask the right question to get the answers to a question you didn't know you needed to ask!

Lights-out comes way too early for us after spending the day sleeping and there's a lot of quiet conversation going on in the tent that night. There's no point talking about any plan right now with no new information so we all just keep quiet and try to doze off. I'm surprised that the two little boys go back to sleep so easily but I guess with all the trauma and upheaval they had been through over the last few days, they were just mentally done in. I'm just glad Benny went to sleep so quickly. I don't have any answers to his many questions and the scared look in his eyes just shreds my heart.

Sleep must have found me because the next thing I know, some soldier is bellowing at us to wake up. I feel groggy and gross and I'd kill for a long hot shower followed by a steaming cup of coffee with a fresh dose of cream from Nods. As I clear the sleep from my eyes, I doubt very much that's ever going to happen. I turn my head to the front of the tent and see a replay of last night. Same boxes and bottles carried in, same clipboard guy.

"ATTENTION! These are your morning rations. One per person! Form two lines by gender to be escorted to the latrines. You have one hour to prepare before you will be assigned your work duties for the day." He gives everyone in the tent a hard look. "There will be NO disobedience or disputing of the assignments. Work duties have been assigned based on the answers to the questions of skills you gave us yesterday. Everyone will comply! After a few days, there may be a reassignment request filed but it will be decided based on need, not want. Anyone not complying with their assignments will be punished with reduced rations to start. Continuing noncompliance will result in harsher punishment." He gives us one more hard glare before barking, "As you were!"

As soon as the guy leaves the tent Lance waves all of us towards him.

"I think we need to just go with the flow for the first few days to see what they have planned for us and how their security is going to manage all these people. I'd say there's around fifty people in this tent and I saw three other tents set up out there so call it two hundred people they have to manage. That's a lot of possible pissed off people if they took some of them by force along the journey to get here. We need to try and get some of the soldiers talking. Find out how many they have and get a feel for their mood. See if they're all onboard with the General's plans. Once we have a better feel for things, we can start trying to come up with an exit plan." He zeroes in on Rex and Marsh. "Boys, that means you need to take whatever they dish out. No matter how much it pisses you off. Our group needs to stay off of their radar until we're ready to make our move. Understand?"

Rex and Marsh clearly aren't happy about it but they both nod in agreement. We all get up and move to either the restroom lines or to grab food and water. I stare down at the nasty MRE's in my hands for Ben and me and think longingly of the fresh eggs and toast I would normally make for us for breakfast. The anger and frustration I feel knowing that Bill and his soldiers will be eating my food instead makes me hope they'll choke on it! When I get back to our cot and see Benny still curled up, I sigh. I'm really worried about him and how he's processing all these awful changes that have been thrown at him so fast.

"Hey, Benny? You can pick which one of these you get for breakfast. Your choices are spaghetti Bolognese or chicken teriyaki with rice." I try and make my tone upbeat but he just gives me a small shrug and rolls over to face the other way. I sit on the side of the cot and place my hand on his back. "Come on, buddy, you have to eat something. It could be worse, the ones with eggs have a green tint to them!" When I still get no response from him, I set the meals and bottles on the floor and stretch out beside him, pulling him close to me. I breathe in the smell of little boy and kiss the back of his head.

"Benny, I need you to help me out here. I know things aren't great right now but I'm begging you to trust me. Me and the others are working on a plan to set things right but we need time to make it happen. I'm not going to be very helpful to them if I'm too busy worrying about you. I really need you to help with this. I promise it'll just be for a few days."

His small shoulders stiffen. "And then we can go back inside? To our home?" He asks in a hopeful tone.

I bite my lip to keep from sighing again. "Benny, you know the plan was always going to be us leaving the bunker to start rebuilding. It's just come faster than I thought it would. Rex and Matty and all the others are going with us to build a new home. Won't it be great to see the sky and the sun every day? And the stars, Benny, we get to look at the stars every night!"

He tries to bury deeper into the cot so his voice is muffled when he speaks. "I don't care about that. I just want to go back inside. I want AIRIA back!"

I give him another kiss on his soft hair and sit up. "I'm sorry but that's not going to happen. I'm sad too but I have to do what's right for us and you need to help me. You aren't the only one who lost their home, you know. How do you think Matty feels? Have you checked if your friend is all right? He could probably use his buddy right now too."

I sit and wait to see if my words have any effect on him and hold in a smile of relief when he sits up and turns my way. He looks past me and sees Matty sitting on his cot with a grossed out look on his face as he peers down into his MRE pouch. Ben looks at the pouch I hold out to him and gives a fake shudder so I use the universal bribe for all children.

"Eat and I'll give you the dessert from mine."

His face changes to cunning. "And the peanut butter and crackers?"

I shake my head at him but my lips tug up into a satisfied smile. "FINE! You con artist!"

His giggle lifts about twenty pounds off my shoulders and settles the knot in my stomach enough to let me eat my own bland meal.

Chapter Seven...Rex

No one is surprised by our work assignments. Ethan is tapped to work in the med clinic, Belle is on childcare which includes Matty and Ben, while the rest of us are on labor. I had seen the large farm equipment being trucked out when I visited the restrooms this morning so I guess they have an area they are going to clear. Our jobs for the day are basically heave, carry, and lift smaller farm tools and boxes and bags of seeds into the back of transport trucks. They have way more trucks than I realized and the sheer amount of supplies amazes even Skylar. She says she should have spent more time going through the lower levels when she had the chance. The work is hard, sweaty and monotonous. No one talks to each other and after a few hours, the people doing the task start to resemble zombies. The only good thing I can say about the day of lifting is that the soldiers mainly ignore us except to give basic directions. They seem almost as bored as us. No one's getting harassed but no one's getting any information either.

We finish the day achy, sweaty and hungry for a meal as we weren't given any lunch rations. As I head back to the tent I'm slowed by the sound of saws and hammers. There are a group of people working on building two long structures. I take a closer look at the materials stacked to the side and see a stack of pipes and boxes with the word faucets stamped on the side and assume that the buildings will be some type of washing rooms. I turn away from the builders hoping they will hurry. I went years without having a daily shower, just sponge baths and the rare full bath heated by pots over the fire but living in the bunker for the last while has spoiled me to the luxury of being fully clean every day.

The evening rations are already set up on the table and after a quick look down the tent to see Matty isn't eating yet, I grab two and our water bottles before joining him and the others. No one talks as we dive into the meals and chug down our water. Today wasn't that physically demanding but if we are assigned anything harder, we will need more water and food to keep up. I think it's funny that I went years with very little food and managed just fine but after eating so much in the bunker my body is feeling starved after only two meals a day.

Ethan joins us just as we are finishing up our meals and sets his own ration aside. I guess working inside gives him the perks of having lunch. After a brief private conversation with Lance, the two motion us in. We all hand over the small packs of candies that come in the MRE's to Ben and Matty to distract them before Lance starts off with a question.

"Anyone have a chance to chat up any of our guards today?"

Belle and Ethan are the only ones to nod their heads so he motions Belle to go first.

"They left two female soldiers in here to monitor us. I'm not sure why though. It's not like we were going to rise up and riot with a bunch of little kids! Anyways, I got one of the women talking but she didn't go into a lot of detail. Just that they were happy to have arrived and have so much space and better food. I got the impression that the bunker they came from in the east was damaged in some way causing them to be stuck in a small area together. When I asked about the whole rebuilding the population thing, she clammed up and kept her distance but not before I saw an eye roll so who knows what that means. The other woman never spoke to us and looked annoyed to be in here the whole time. The only positive thing was that the nice one went and got us a few pitchers of juice and bread with peanut butter for the kids at lunch but that could have been just to keep them quiet for a little while. I did suggest they bring out some learning materials or games at least to keep the kids occupied."

Ethan nods his head. "Yes, the only doctor they have, Dr. Craven, was a fountain of information. It was like he was starved for company. He told me that their bunker was damaged on the very first day when the bombs dropped forcing them all into the lower levels. A lot of their supplies were contaminated and they weren't able to grow as much fresh food as they needed. He said they lost over forty percent of their personnel to suicide and internal violence before they could leave to head this way. I'm guessing that's why the General is keeping us around for labor.

He also told me that he hopes the General holds off on his plans for forced breeding because the female soldiers have already been forced to accommodate many of the male soldiers sexually and often without consent. The doctor feels that the morale of many of the soldiers is already too low and forcing that on them will cause desertion or worse, civil war." He looks to each of us with a grim expression. "We do not want to be anywhere near these guys if they decide to go to war with each other. With no weapons or allies, we would be cannon fodder. The good news is that none of that will happen until after the farming gets started up. They sent equipment out today to clear the land they plan to use and tomorrow you guys will be sent out to start hand planting the vegetable crops. They have some ambitious plans for wheat, corn and soy crops that the machines will handle but all the vegetable crops will be done by hand. Once everything is in the ground, the doctor expects the General to turn his sights to the population program."

No one looks happy to hear this news but we have no choice but to go along for now. Lance gives a sharp nod. "Alright, can you prod the doctor to make sure they're giving us more than two meals and two bottles of water a day? It's not exactly hot out here but we will need more water for sure if we are out working the fields." At Ethan's nod of agreement, he continues. "The rest of us need to keep our eyes open and watch everything. How the guards are deployed, how many, possible weaknesses we can use and anything else that might help us. Also, keep trying to get them talking. If they've been stuck together in a tight space for the last seven years, someone is going to want to chat with someone new. Girls, talk to as many of the other female soldiers as you can. There's cracks out there we can use, we just have to find them."

There's not much to say after that so we finish our meals and carry our garbage to the bin at the front of the tent. I'm tired and I just want to rack out and go to sleep but after spending the whole day away from Matty I feel like I should spend some time with him. Skylar must be feeling the same way about Ben so we grab the two monkeys and play a couple of rousing games of I Spy until there's absolutely nothing else we could possibly pick in the limited décor of the tent. Lights-out comes quickly after that and as I close my eyes, I wonder if tomorrow will be the day that gives us the information we need to make a break from this place.

I wake briefly in the night when distant yelling rouses me followed by two gunshots. Others stir around me but no one gets up as we all wait to see if the commotion will move closer to our tent. After five minutes of quiet, I drift back to sleep.

Matty's sharp-elbow digs into my stomach, waking me the next morning with a groan. As much as I love having the little guy close to me, his lanky body is growing by the day and I'm going to have to find a new cot for him if either one of us is going to have a comfortable sleep for much longer. He desperately needs to use the bathroom so I push myself up off the cot to see if one of the guards is around to take us when I see Benny's eyes are open and he's wiggling around as well. I motion for him to stand up with us. Hopefully, Skylar will be able to get a few more minutes of sleep before we have to start our day. The guard is nodding off in a chair beside the table at the front of the tent so I try not to startle him too badly when I whisper our need to him. He shakes the sleep from his eyes and stands up while waving us towards the flaps.

As we walk to the porta-potties, I take a good look at the half-completed bathhouses they're building and hope that they'll be usable by the time we finish our day in the fields. Glancing towards the other tents my steps slow when I see two black and occupied body bags in front of the furthest one. Whatever went down last night caused at least two people to lose their lives.

Once everyone's needs are taken care of we head back into the tent but I see no one has stirred since we left. I know there's no way these two boys are going to go back to sleep. They just haven't burned off enough energy being stuck in the tent for the last couple of days. I get the guards attention and motion to a spot on the floor behind the table and he nods his head in agreement.

"Okay boys, if we sit up here and you're quiet I'll tell you a story."

They both eagerly nod their heads and settle down onto the ground, looking at me expectantly so I start to weave a story in a low voice about an orphan boy who lives on a desert planet. When one day when he's out doing his chores, he comes across an incredible little machine called a Droid that he rescues and becomes fast friends with. I tell them the tale of the boy growing into a man as he leaves his planet in search of a princess that he needs to rescue. Halfway through the story I glanced up and see the smile on the guard's face so I lift my chin to him to encourage him to participate and he proceeds to tell the boys all about the evil empire and how they have a massive death machine that will destroy whole planets. By the time we come to the end of the first chapter of the story the four of us are thoroughly entertained and the people in the tent are starting to stir.

When I see Skylar sit up on her cot looking around frantically, I push to my feet and pull the boys up with me sending them back down to where our people are. I turn to the guard and shoot him a look of gratitude.

"Thanks, man, that was nice to be able to give them a little bit of an escape. They're bored out of their minds stuck in here."

The grin is still plastered across his face when he nods back. "Yeah man, that was great! Those used to be my favorite movies growing up. It was nice to revisit them. I wonder if we'll ever be able to see those movies again someday."

I give a half shrug and say, "I'm sure AIRIA has that whole series in her data banks. You could always request it for a movie night in the barracks."

The guy looks at me with confusion for a minute before shaking his head. "Movie night? For some reason, I don't think that's going to play into the General's plans. He's not real big on entertainment."

Before I can reply the flaps are shoved open and another soldier comes in followed by others carrying our morning rations and water. The guy I was talking to straightens up and turns his back on me like I was never there in the first place. I sigh and then head back to our cots so the guy won't get into trouble for talking to the enemy.

Breakfast is over quickly and minutes later were rounded up and loaded into the back of a troop transport truck. There's a whole line of trucks filled with the things that we had loaded the day before as well as people and soldiers ready to go to wherever they've picked to do the farming.

I give Skylar a hand up into the back of our truck and the smile she sends my way has my stomach fluttering and my head cursing her uncle for showing up just as the two of us were starting to build a deeper relationship. It feels like Sky and I have gone from crisis to crisis and I'm dying for the chance just to be with her in a semi-normal setting so we can build on what we had started. The way it looks now, that won't happen for the foreseeable future.

Chapter Eight...Skylar

There's bench seating around the sides and the front of the truck bed and I make my way to the very front and settle onto the bench. There's a male and female guard sitting with their backs to the cab of the truck with bored expressions on their faces. Rex settles across from me while the rest of our people find their seats down the sides of the truck. There's not enough seating for everybody that they're cramming into the truck so some people are forced to sit on the hard floor of the truck bed.

As soon as the back gate is closed the large diesel engines rumble to life and within a few minutes we're lurching ahead. It's slow going at first as we make our way through the trees and over many bumps until we hit the road that turns south towards the town of Canmore. I lose myself in thoughts of the last time I was in town and wonder if it'll look any different now. When I left the hotel where we found Rex and Sasha it was a raging inferno and I wonder if the fire was contained or if it ran unchecked through the town. I hope my dad's truck was far enough away that it wasn't damaged if the fire was out of control. We might need that vehicle in the near future to escape from my uncle.

I keep my eyes peeled for the access road that we had parked the truck down. When we pass it, I'm relieved to see that it's lined with dead but not burnt trees. If the fire was out of control, it didn't reach this far. We take the overpass before exiting onto the highway, giving us a good view of the town and it's easy to see that the fire stayed contained to the hotel as none of the other buildings look damaged. Once we're on the highway, we pick up speed quickly. Most of the cars that had been abandoned on it the day of the bombs have already been pushed to the side.

I turn away from the dead and empty town and glance at the people around me, catching movement by the male guard that sits in front of me. He's pulled a plastic wrapped egg from one of his pockets and precedes to start peeling the shell from it.

Rex speaks up, breaking my stare. "Hey, Skylar. Looks like your chickens survived."

The soldier looks up from his egg towards Rex and then me with a confused look on his face, so Rex explains.

"Yeah, those eggs you're eating came from Skylar's chickens."

The female soldier leans forward and breaks into the conversation. "You had chickens? How on earth did you manage to keep chickens alive all these years?"

I give her a small smile. "It wasn't all that hard. They live a pretty comfortable life inside the bunker. I hope whoever is taking care of them is saving eggs to make more baby chicks now that there's so many more mouths to feed."

The woman looks at her partner and then back to me. "You lived inside the bunker?" When I just nod my head she asks, "How'd you get in there?"

I meet her eyes dead on. "My mom and dad and I went there the day the bombs dropped."

Her eyes flare wide in surprise. "You and your family have been living inside the bunker this whole time?"

I give a tiny shake of my head. "Not all of us. My mom died the first day after giving birth to my little brother and then my dad died a couple years after that. Then it was just me and my little brother Ben."

Her eyes go sad and she gives a small shake of her head. "You've been in there all alone with a little kid this whole time? How old were you when your dad died?"

I swallow back the sadness that fills me at the thought of the day when my father died and left us all alone but push it aside and reply, "I had just turned thirteen when he died. Ben was not quite three years old."

She opens her mouth to ask another question when her partner interrupts.

"Megan, I don't think we're supposed to be talking to them this much."

We both spear him with a look but it's Megan who scoffs.

"Really, Tony? So what, then? We're all going to work at rebuilding this area and try to get back to some kind of normal lives but we're never going to talk to anyone who isn't in a uniform? How's that supposed to work?"

He flushes red, gives a half-hearted shrug and looks away, so Megan turns back to me with an eye roll. I like this lady!

"So you were all alone with a toddler for years? How did you manage that without going insane?" she asks.

I give a small laugh. "Well, the jury's still out on the sanity part but I had AIRIA to walk and talk me through a lot of it. She was sort of a mother, father and teacher all rolled into one. She kept me on track for the most part."

Megan leans back and lets out a breath of semi-disbelief. "Still, it must have been incredibly lonely in that huge barracks with just a tiny kid for company."

I shake my head. "No, we had our own living quarters that my Dad built beside the main barracks. He made it a replica of our house in the city. Behind that we had our own cavern with a farm and storage area. I didn't even know Uncle Bill had built the barracks next door until after my dad died and AIRIA increases my clearance level to green."

This last bit gets Tony's attention and he blurts out, "Uncle Bill? General Mallor's your uncle?"

I lift a shoulder. "Godfather, actually. He and my dad served together and stayed close after my dad mustered out."

He shakes his head in confusion. "Then what are you doing out here? If you have your own place inside, why didn't you stay in there?"

I give him a hard look. "Evicted. Good old Uncle Bill took one look at the place my dad built and decided it would be his new home. I guess they weren't as good of friends as my dad thought."

"Wow, that's harsh! But not really surprising considering how he treats his own son." He says with a grimace.

Megan's tone is far harsher. "He's a right bastard!"

Tony whips his head towards her. "Hey, he might not be very nice but he kept us alive for the last seven years. You could have faced a lot worse without him!"

She turns to him and scowls. "Oh yeah, it was a right picnic for you boys. Too bad it wasn't so great for us girls! There's a reason we lost so many women to suicide, Tony, but yeah, thank god the General saved us." She throws up her hands and does air quotes when she says the word saved.

His back goes stiff and his face is blank when he barks at her. "That's enough chit-chat, Private!"

Her own expression turns to stone. "Sir, yes Sir!"

When she turns away from him, I catch the suppressed rage in her eyes and swear I hear the sound of a crack widening. I look over to Rex and see him lean back with a neutral expression but there's a glint of satisfaction in his eyes. I have to turn away to keep from smiling. He sure is cute when he's stirring the pot!

I watch the landscape go by instead. We've left the mountains and are now traveling through the foothills. We're just coming up to an exit and I see a single Hummer leave the convoy and take the exit. I can just make out the faded white letters on the equally faded green highway sign that says Kananaskis. I follow the Hummer with my eyes for as long as

I can, wishing that was me. I wish I could just load up Ben, Rex, Matty and all the others into my dad's truck and drive away. Go explore the world now that the skies have cleared and pick out a new home. It's going to happen, I'm sure of it. We just have to find the right moment to make it happen.

It isn't long before we leave the foothills and the wide-open prairies spread out before us. The sky is huge here and my stomach rolls a bit at so much open space but it's the ground and what the tires are kicking up that sickens me.

As far as the eye can see, the fields, trees, and buildings have been burnt. The landscape is completely black or gray from soot and ash. Every time the wind blows, it sends clouds of it billowing into the air. My eyes quickly start to burn and my lungs protest with a hacking cough. Everyone in the back of the truck is suffering along with me except for the guards who were quick to don goggles and filter masks. I spend the rest of the ride with my shirt pulled up over my face for protection, cursing these fracking people and wishing I was in that lone Hummer speeding away.

Chapter Nine...Joslin

"Why are we doing this again?" Jackson asks in annoyance as he drives us away from the convoy.

I spear him with a look. "I'm sorry, do you have something more interesting to do? Are you really that eager to stand around watching those poor people being worked like slaves? Or maybe you love hanging out with the same people we've been stuck with for the last seven years?" I say with sarcasm. When he makes no reply, I sigh. "Come on, Jacks! Here's our chance to explore and get away from them for a while. We can see something new and besides, I did an overflight of the area with the drones and found some interesting places that might give us some good scavenge."

He glances away from the road ahead to me and gives a tentative smile. "You know what, it will be nice to get away for a bit."

I smile in relief. I'm not ready to share my real plans with him yet but it's imperative that I get a grounds-eye view of the places I saw on the drone footage. I need to have all my ducks in a row before I make a move that will change everything. Until then, I need to keep my cards close to my chest. I want Jackson with me but I'll need a strong case to sway him for going against his dad. It doesn't matter how hard the General is on him, he's still Jackson's only family and it will take a lot to break that bond.

We drive in silence as we take in the dead forest surrounding the road. I'm happy the General stopped his burn program before we reached this point or we would have had to find a reason to go even further away to find what I think we will need.

Jackson slows down as signs start appearing so we can read the faded words that point first to a turn off to a ski hill and then to what was once a luxury hotel with a nearby golf course. The property will have a lot of the resources I think we will need, but it's huge, and what I'm really interested in lies at the next junction in the road so I wave Jackson forward.

"We can stop on the way back and check out the hotel. The turn we want should only be a few more minutes ahead."

Thankfully, he doesn't protest again and just keeps driving before turning when I point at the road I'm interested in. He pulls up and stops in front of an open gate with a pair of matching totem poles flanking the opening. Each totem pole is the anchor to the start of an old fort style log wall that is over twelve feet tall and from what I saw on the drone cameras, wraps around the entire property. I study the entrance closely while ignoring the incredulous look Jackson has sent my way. He finally loses his patience.

"A summer camp? What the heck would we need from a summer camp that we don't already have in the bunker's storage?"

I give him an impish grin. "Nothing really, but I always wanted to go to one of these places on school break but none of my foster families were willing to pay for it." I give him my best pitiful look. "Please Jackson? I just want to look around! When I saw it on the drone feed, I couldn't resist the idea. It might be my only chance to ever see one!"

He gives an amused shake of his head but starts rolling through the gates. I hate deceiving my best…my only…friend this way. Hopefully, it will be worth it if my plans fall into place.

He parks in front of the biggest building and shuts the Hummer down before turning expectantly to me. I send him a gleeful grin before shoving out of the vehicle and bouncing up the stairs. I'm concerned that the double front doors will be locked and I'll have to break the glass to get in but after a few tugs, they part for me. The wall is number two on my list of must-haves but there are two other needs that are just as important for this to work so I delve deeper into the dim building and find another yes on the list.

The room opens up with sunlight flooding through the atrium above showing me a huge central fireplace with a large vent above that rises up to the ceiling. There are benches ringing the fireplace with room to sit at least fifty people.

Jackson comes in and joins me with an arched eyebrow so I add to the deception by asking in a wistful tone, "Do you think the campers sang camp songs and made smores in here when the weather was bad?"

He reaches over and pats my back in sympathy. "I'm sorry you never got to do all things you should have been able to do before the bombs, Joss. I wish things could have been different for you."

I give him a genuine smile for his sweetness and then shrug. "It is what it is. Hopefully, the future will give me a chance at some of the things I missed out on. Come on, let's go check out some of the cabins!"

He gives me a concerned, thoughtful look but nods and follows me out of the building. That's good. I want him thinking about what a crappy future I will have under his dad's thumb.

We spend a few minutes in each of the camper's cabins but they're pretty bare bones with just bunks and moth-eaten blankets covering them. Some of the cabins have been exposed to the elements and wildlife have gotten into a few, making big messes. I keep my eyes peeled as we move through the camp for the final thing that I need to make this location work and finally spot it just as Jackson starts to lose interest. There's an outdoor shower area set up near the small stream that runs along the back wall of the camp and I head right for it when I see the distinct handle sticking out of the ground. It's fused with rust but I keep trying to get it to move until finally I give up and yell for Jackson.

He comes over and shakes his head. "What are you doing?"

I blow out a breath of frustration. "Can you just please help me to get this pump working? I want to see if there's still water here!"

He crosses his arms and spears me with a look. "Why?"

I match his stance and cock my head towards the pump. He might be twice my size but I'm twice as stubborn as he is so it only takes half a minute for him to throw up his arms in concession. I watch in annoyance as he kicks the handle twice and gets it moving. He's bulked up in the last few years with all the training his dad makes him do and it only takes him five pumps for the water I was hoping for to gush out of the shower head.

Inside I'm overjoyed to check the last box on my list but all I say is, "Cool, thanks!" And turn away to head back to the Hummer.

He catches up to me quickly, grabs my arm and says with exasperation, "Joss, what are we really doing here?"

I bite my lip before replying and answer his question with one of my own.

"What do you think of Skylar?"

He narrows his eyes at my misdirection but drops my arm.

"She's fierce and furious. Not that I blame her after what my dad pulled on her." He kicks at the ground with the toe of his boot. "I don't know why he has to be such a hard-ass all the time! He didn't have to kick her and the kid out of their home. There's plenty of room on the other side for all of us. It's like he needs to constantly rub everyone's nose in the fact that he's the boss. I get so sick of it."

I make an agreeable hum in the back of my throat before saying, "You know it's going to get worse, right? He's going to work those people to the bone and once everything is planted, start on the breeding program. That means that Skylar and every woman, both outside and in, will be forced to have babies, year after year. That includes me! And what do you think the chances are that we'll get to pick who our baby daddies are?" At his look of disbelief, I snort. "Seriously? I've seen the spreadsheets he had the doc make up! It's all about population diversification. Lots of babies with lots of daddies!"

His face is pale when he gives his head a hard shake. "He wouldn't do that! I'll talk to him. Make him see reason!"

I reach out and grab his hand and say with compassion, "No offense, Jackson, but when was the last time anything you said swayed your dad?"

His face crumples. "Then what are we supposed to do? I can't sit by and watch that happen to you or anyone for that matter!"

His expression is so filled with hopelessness that I take a chance.

"We could leave! Find a new home and start our own rebuilding. I'm sure there's others that feel the same way that would join us. The skies have cleared. Now's the time for us to start building a future for US, not for him!"

I see hope cross his face for a split second before he frowns and shakes his head.

"We both know he would never let us or anyone go. He's too powerful, especially now that he has AIRIA to track us with the drones. He'd catch us in a day and then punish us with a life even worse than the one we have now."

I want to rant at his cowardice but I know that won't win him to my side so I stay silent and wait as he spins away from me and looks over the camp.

"So was this your plan? This place?" He asks with his back to me.

I walk around to speak to him face to face and make my case.

"The wall gives us a barrier of protection we can defend. The well is still flowing for water and the atrium gives us a place to grow crops inside as well as out here. The nearby hotel will give us resources to scavenge. All we need to do is start siphoning off supplies from the bunker to get us through a year or two until we can be self-sufficient. We would need weapons, seeds, and MRE's to start. If we can get enough people to come with us, we could grow here and defend it!"

He looks around again. "And when the General comes after us with those still loyal to him? A lot of people will die!"

My face firms up in determination. "Jackson, I survived the first eight years of my life as an inconvenience to every person around me. I survived the first three years in the bunker by hiding and I survived the last four years under your father's thumb, forced to be his lackey spy. I had no choice in any of that but now that the skies have cleared, I do have a choice and it sure as frack isn't going to be surviving as his broodmare! I choose not to survive anymore but to LIVE!" The last word explodes out of me with all the pent-up emotion that I've been forced to suppress for the last seventeen years causing Jackson to take a step back from me. I spin away from him and give him my back. "I want you to come *live* with me but I'm ready to do it alone if I have too."

I don't wait for a response from him. I stride towards the Hummer, trying to get my emotions under control. I've kept that door tightly locked for many years and it's served me well. I can't let something as basic as feelings derail me now.

By the time I slam the door to the Hummer closed, I have a big old padlock on the door in my mind and I start to worry about how Jackson will respond to what I said. If he shares any of my plan with his father, this plan will be over before it even starts and that will mean my only option will have to be a direct assault on the General and everyone who supports him. It would be very messy and I would be in a lot of danger, even with AIRIA under my control.

He gets in the Hummer and starts it up without saying a word, making me clutch my hands tight in my lap so I don't gnaw on my nails in worry. He puts the vehicle in gear but doesn't press the gas. Instead, he lets out a deep sigh. I keep my face turned to the window as he begins to speak.

"I'm sorry. I'm sorry that you've had such a hard life, Joss. I'll help you. I'll help move as many supplies as I can to give you the best shot at surv…living, I mean. I'd like to think that when the time comes I'll go with you but I don't know if I'm strong enough to leave him."

I finally turn to my friend. "Thank you, Jackson. I just have to ask, I mean, if you say anything to your Dad about this…"

A hurt look crosses his face as he shakes his head. "I wouldn't do that to you! You're my best friend, Joss. I'd do anything for you, even let you go."

Even as I nod in gratitude, I feel a part of my heart break. By the time I'm done with my plan, he will either come with me willingly or hate me forever. Maybe both.

Chapter Ten...Skylar

Everything hurts. My eyes burn and feel swollen and full of scratches. My back aches like I've been laying on a bed of pointy rocks and some of the blisters on my hands are the size of grapes that weep a clear fluid every time I try and stretch them from the curled swollen paws they resemble. I can't stop coughing as my lungs try and expel some of the ash and soot that they were forced to breathe in all day. Each cough brings another round of aches as my abused muscles brace against it. When the wind stops blowing ash against my shirt, I lower it, crack my puffy eyes and blow out a breath of relief when I see that we're climbing through the trees on the way to the bunker. Almost...home, or at least almost to my tent that's now my home. I didn't think this day would ever end and I just can't fathom how any of us are going to be physically able to do it all again tomorrow.

I slowly turn my head and scan the others in the truck bed. Some of them are better off than me and some are worse. Lance, Marsh and Rex look wiped out but not as bad off. They've been living in the outdoors for years and have conditioned their bodies to chop huge amounts of wood, giving them the calluses needed to protect the skin on their hands. Sasha, on the other hand, looks almost catatonic. I turn the other way and glance at the guards. Even if I had the energy to try and engage some of them, I would fail because they won't look at any of us. I don't know if it's because they no longer see us as people worth talking to or if they're ashamed of what we were forced to endure in those fields.

The guy in charge of the work group today must be a sadistic bastard because he didn't let up on us all day long. His name is Donnelly and he barked at us constantly to keep moving, keep digging and his favorite, get up! Other than twice receiving water, we worked from the moment we unloaded from the truck until the sun started to go down. You'd think with just under two hundred people we would have made huge progress but I only managed to plant two rows and barely that. When they cleared the field of the contaminated topsoil they neglected to go back over it with a tiller to loosen the soil up for planting, leaving a hard-packed level that needed to be tilled by hand with shovels and axes to loosen the soil enough to plant anything. It was backbreaking work especially for people who haven't been doing much physical activity in years.

I'm looking at my blackened palms and the curls of skin that hang from them from where blisters have broken when I hear Rex groan, causing me to lift my head up to meet his gaze in question. He tilts his head back and closes his eyes while he answers me.

"I was hoping they'd have the wash houses done by the time we got back."

I lean to the side and see that we've arrived back at the bunker but there are two trucks of people ahead of us to unload before it's our turn. I look over to the construction area and see that the wash houses are no more than half-done. It just makes me more tired knowing that there won't be a way to get clean of the ash, soot, and dirt before laying down for the night. I close my eyes again while we wait but a minute later there's some kind of ruckus happening with people yelling up at the front of the line.

"That's Ethan," Lance says with a slight smile. "Always doctoring."

Our truck moves up to the next spot in line getting us closer to all the yelling and I can now make out words.

"You get him out here right now!" Is what I hear before I see Ethan stagger to the side of the next truck. I push to my feet in concern as fast as my body will allow when I see another soldier rush towards him but sag in relief when he just reaches down and helps Ethan to his feet again. They both disappear behind the truck but the yelling has stopped so I slowly lower myself back down.

Lance looks to me as he's on the other side of the bed without a view.

"Looked like someone hit or shoved him but he's ok."

Lance's lips flatten into a hard line but all he does is nod. It sucks, but it was his plan to take what they dish out and not fight back until we're ready to make our move. The truck lurches ahead minutes later and I can't wait to get somewhere I can just lie down flat on. The gate is opened and I watch as people stagger, fall and slide out the back until it is our turn. Lance and Marsh have to lift Sasha to her feet to get her moving and I stand behind them with Rex as they lower her gently into Ethan's arms before hopping down themselves. I have no hope left in me so I just lower myself to my butt and prepare to slide off the end when a harsh voice rings out.

"What was SO important that I had to come out here?"

I look up from my dangling feet to see the thunderous expression of Uncle Bill as he strides towards us and decide to stay put to see what plays out. The soldier who had helped Ethan to his feet whirls around to face him.

"Look at this! Look at the condition of these people!" He yells in indignation.

The General looks around at the workers sitting or lying down on the ground and gives an indifferent shrug. "Your point?"

The soldier, who I think is the doctor Ethan's been working with throws his hands into the air in frustration. "My point? My point is they should have been given gloves and goggles at least to protect them from the environment as well as food, more water and rest. They were worked so hard that many of them are flat out broken!"

I'm watching my uncle's face so I see the flash of satisfaction cross his eyes before they return to annoyance. He did this on purpose. He wanted us to suffer so that we'd be put in our place and not have the energy or the will to cause him any problems. He is a monster and it just fuels me to escape from here and from him. As if he's heard my thoughts, his eyes find mine as I sit at the end of the truck bed and he scans me up and down focusing for a moment on the damaged hands I clutch to my chest. Just as fast, he dismisses me and looks back to the doctor.

"You can't make an omelet without cracking a few eggs, Craven. The crops need to be planted if we want to get a harvest before the weather turns again. Did you think rebuilding would be easy?" He sneers.

Doctor Craven shakes his head in disbelief. "Bill, none of us will be eating that omelet if you pulverize all the eggs first! They can't go at this pace, especially without the proper gear."

The General studies the doctor for a moment before giving him a nod. "Fine, do what you need to do to fix them up and I'll have Donnelly adjust the schedule." He turns to leave but not before I catch the small, smug smile that tugs at his lips. Oh yeah, this was totally his plan all along. Grind them into the dust then look like a savior by helping them up. If I had my guns right now, I wouldn't hesitate for a second to empty every bullet into him.

I shove off of the back of the truck bed and slide to the ground. Anger has pushed aside my weariness giving me the strength to try and help some of the people on the ground to their feet. The doctor and Ethan are leading the workers towards the huge barrack doors that the doctor ordered opened. Dr. Craven is yelling orders to some of the soldiers that are milling around to fetch him medical supplies and fresh clothing and towels as he has us line up by gender at the shower room doors.

I take Sasha from Lance and Marsh and get into line, leaning her against the wall with a steadying hand to keep her upright. While we wait for our turn in the shower, I scan the barracks that I had to myself for so many years and see that all the changes Rex and his people had done when they moved in have been reversed. All the bunks are back in their original places and there are no more sheets up to give privacy. There are a lot of soldiers standing around staring at us. Some of them have expressions filled with sympathy or pity. Some are indifferent and some are annoyed. I tilt my head back against the wall and close my sore eyes so I don't have to look at any of them. Frack them. Frack them all!

"Skylar, Sasha?" Brings me out of the half-doze I've fallen into while standing against the wall. Ethan's in front of me holding out his hand but I have to blink a few times for my sight to clear enough to see that he's holding out a palm filled with pain relievers. I have to force my stiff, swollen fingers open to take three of the beauties from him and dry swallow them. He pulls my hands towards him and winces before doing the same with Sasha's.

"As soon as you're finished showering, I'll get some ointment and bandages on these. You'll need to try and not use them as best as you can for a while."

I huff out a laugh. "Really? Ok, I just let the men with the big guns know I'll be taking the rest of the week off. Do you think they'll dock my pay?"

He smiles at my attempt at humor and pats my arm. "There won't be any work for a few days. The General made his point so now he'll let all of you rest before sending you out again."

I arch my eyebrows. "Caught that too?"

He rolls his eyes. "He's a classic dictator bully. I'm sure he has a perfectly crafted playbook in his pocket for how to subject people to his will. This won't be the last game he plays with us."

I sigh in agreement and look over his shoulder. Standing not far away are Jackson and Joslin. While his expression is filled a mix of disbelief and outrage as he looks over the state we're all in, Joslin is staring right at me with a look of determination. It's almost like she is trying to tell me something with her eyes but I'm just too tired to figure it out and to be honest, she creeps me out a little bit with the way she looks at me like she knows me.

The woman beside me stirs with a groan and shuffles through the shower room door breaking my attention from the weird girl so I nod my thanks to Ethan and pull Sasha with me into the shower room. The warm moist air seems to perk her up and she steadies on her feet before grabbing a towel from the stack and rushing to an open stall. I move a little slower than her. As much as I know the hot water will feel amazing on my sore muscles, I also know it's going to really hurt my damaged hands to soap up.

Peeling my clothes off is a challenge in itself and I stare down at the gross heap of them and consider bringing them into the shower with me to clean. I don't have an unlimited supply anymore and I don't want to give them up but there's no way I'll be able to wring the water from them with my hands in this condition so I just leave them on the floor. At first, I just stand under the hot spray and let the nasty ash and soot wash off of me but I need soap so I grit my teeth against the pain and just go for it. Judging by the sounds coming from the stalls around me, I'm not the only one suffering. I just hope the pain pills kick in soon to take the edge off.

By the time I'm clean, all the comforting that I would have gotten from the hot water is lost to the extreme pain from my throbbing hands. It takes three times as long to dry off and get the fresh clothes that have been left in a stack, back on my body. I'm practically asleep on my feet as I stagger out the door and take my place back in line against the wall to wait for my turn to have my hands treated. I can't even stay on my feet this time so I just slide down the wall until my butt hits the floor and I close my eyes.

I don't know how long I sit there but when I feel a hand on my leg and open my eyes I see that most of the line is gone. There are only six people left to be treated and none of them are near me. I turn my head, expecting Ethan to be in front of me but instead find Joslin there with a medkit in her hands. I'm just too tired to care so I give her a blank stare and hold my open hands out to her.

She grimaces down at them but opens the kit, pulls out tiny scissors and starts snipping away the peeling skin. He voice is low as she keeps her eyes on my hands.

"I volunteered to help. I was hoping for a chance to talk to you alone."

I grunt, "Good for you. Why? What do you want from me?"

She glances around quickly to make sure we're still alone and finally meets my eyes.

"I'm going to get you, Benny and your friends the frack out of here!"

What the hell? How is this girl so familiar with how I talk and what I call my little brother? I jerk my hand from hers.

"How do you know that word? Frack?"

A slight smile tugs at her lips but all she says is, "Starbuck."

I'm slightly surprised. "You watched that show?"

She nods. "I've watched all the same shows as you."

Ok, super creepy so I fire back. "Stalker much?"

She blushes in embarrassment and takes my hand back to cover it with ointment.

"The General made me watch footage of you and your brother for years. Both bunkers were linked through AIRIA. He wanted to keep tabs on what was happening here after your dad died."

I hiss in outrage. No longer creeped out, I'm furious.

"You spied on me? For years, you've been spying on me every day?"

She keeps her eyes down and switches hands. "Yes, but it's not like I had any choice in the matter. If it wasn't me, it would have been one of his flunkies. Better to have me than some old guy watching you! If I hadn't spent thousands of hours getting to know you, your brother and your friends you wouldn't have me as an ally. Trust me, as distasteful as me watching you might seem to you, it's going to work out in your favor."

I can't even process the idea of all the things she's seen over the years while watching me. All the ups and down. The small joys and huge heartbreaks? It's like she's peeled me open and exposed everything that I am so I shove it ruthlessly aside to deal with later and focus on the now.

"So, you're going to get us out of here? How? Are you magically going to take down those drones that will track us the minute we make a break from here?

She finishes wrapping my second hand and pats it before leaning back on her heels, looks me dead in the eye and simply says, "Yes."

When she doesn't elaborate, I scoff, "Really? You want to tell me how one girl my age surrounded by soldiers managed to get the power to do that?"

She cocks her head thoughtfully. "He forgot to take away my access." She pauses for a second and her face goes hard. "He also underestimated me."

I shake my head in confusion. "Who are you?" I ask.

Her eyes seem to lose focus like she's gone far away but her whisper is clear.

"I'm his downfall."

Interlude Two
AIRIA EAST

Seven years ago...
Joslin

When we were forced down into the lower levels, I kept my eyes peeled for Jackson but I never saw him or his dad. The woman that was assigned to be my mentor, Captain Marie Cote, has even less patience dealing with me down here than she did above. She keeps one hand clutched around the collar of my shirt as she pulls me through the stacks of shipping pallets and containers until she finds a corner out of the way and thrusts me towards it.

"I want you to stay right here. Do not wander around or leave this area until I return. Once things get organized, we will find a place to set up our bedding. Do you understand?" She asks in a distracted voice as she looks over her shoulder.

My voice is barely a whisper when I agree but she must hear me or she just doesn't care because she turns and strides away. I sit there for hours clutching my backpack and plastic bag full of bedding, waiting for her to come back to tell me where to go. My mind can't stop thinking about the tablet in my pack and the video footage it has of what went down outside. Half of me is desperate to look at it but the other half is just as desperate to not see what I already know happened so I leave it in my pack. I can't see what's happening on this level with pallets blocking the way but I can hear plenty of movement and loud voices calling out instructions. The smell of exhaust is in the air as forklifts move pallets to create space for the soldiers to set up living areas and relocate the supplies from the top level but none come near where I'm hiding. After sitting there undisturbed for hours, my eyes start to droop so I open my plastic bag and retrieve the flattened pillow and a blanket and lay down against the wall. I let sleep take me away but my dreams are filled with the sound of gunfire.

The corner becomes my home for the next two weeks when Captain Cote and three other female soldiers join me in the hidden area with mattresses that had been brought down from the barracks before it was sealed off. There's just enough room behind the row of pallets for our beds to run head to foot down the wall with a small space to walk beside them. We spend ninety percent of our time sitting on our mattresses waiting for the renovations to be completed on this level. It was never meant to house people so the soldiers have to build a food service area and expand the two restrooms so that they can handle the large population. Even with the soldiers split between three lower levels, the restrooms weren't meant to handle this many people and neither one of them had showers in them.

For the first week, we only leave our area to stand in the long restroom lines and to receive our daily rations that they give us first thing in the morning to last the whole day. We wait in boredom and uncertainty for the changes to be made and some kind of schedule to be put in place to fill our days. The other four women in my area mainly ignore me after the first round of questions about who I am and how I ended up here. There's not a lot to talk about after that so they spend most of the time sleeping or staring off into space, lost in the memories of their loved ones that are now likely gone.

By the end of the first week, things start changing as projects are wrapped up. There's a huge area in the center of the level that has been cleared for them to start training with ground mats and exercise equipment along one side of it. Meal times expand to picking up rations three times a day instead of all at once in the morning with the promise of real hot food coming soon instead of the bland MRE's. The major change is the attitude of the people. The shock of what's happened has worn off and they start thinking of what the many years ahead will be like stuck in this bunker. Tempers flare causing heated arguments and sometimes violence. There's so much tension on the level and every time I leave my area I see faces that are filled with hopelessness or anger. By the end of the second week, I'm forced to clutch the pillow around my ears at night to block out the horrible sounds of weeping and worse that are becoming more frequent.

On my last night in the corner, I wake in the middle of the night with a desperate need to use the restroom. I try and ignore it and go back to sleep but it's not happening so I throw back my blanket and quietly try to move past the other mattresses but my foot connects with someone's arm laying in the tight aisle. I freeze with my eyes squeezed shut but whoever I kicked with my foot doesn't wake so I carefully step over it and move on. Most of the lights are turned out at night, so it isn't hard for me to keep to the shadows and avoid running into anyone. I make a dash to the first door of the two options on this level and push the door open. Right away I see a male soldier sitting on the ground with his back against the far wall. He's sobbing into his hands and doesn't see me so I back out and let the door close on his misery. Privacy is at a premium with so many people crammed into the levels so I don't want to disturb the little bit that the poor man has found.

I rush to the next door but it swings open just as I reach it. A woman stands in my way with a swollen eye that will soon be ringed with a black bruise and a split lip that trickles blood. She looks right through me as if I'm not there as she slides past me, letting me get a view of a man without a shirt washing his hands at the sink. Once again, I quickly back away from the door. If that guy did the damage to the woman's face, I don't want to be anywhere near him. I decide that my bladder will just have to wait until morning when things will be slightly safer and turn back. This time I make a straight shot across the main training area where the lights are brightest, no longer trusting the shadows. I just want to get back to my mattress and bury my head and wail with despair at the sad state of things on this level. I haven't seen the General in two weeks and as far as I can tell, there's next to no leadership keeping things under control down here.

I'm in such a rush to get to my mattress that I forget the arm I kicked earlier and end up stepping right on it this time causing me to lose my balance and topple directly onto the person I stepped on. The breath whooshes out of me and it takes a few seconds for me to start apologizing as I try and push myself up and off. My instincts start screaming before my head catches up to the realization that the person I'm on top off hasn't reacted at all to being stepped on and then crashed into. A mewling starts up in my throat as I reach my hand out to the person's face and touch her cheek but it doesn't feel like a normal cheek. It's cool and slightly rubbery making my skin crawl and my stomach roll. The noise I'm making gets louder and changes to a sobbing hiccup.

A beam of a flashlight flares to life and waves around the area until it lands on me, lighting up the empty face and eyes of Captain Cote inches away from mine. I shove off as hard as I can and lunge off of her to land painfully on the concrete floor beside her mattress. The light is like a spotlight that stays on her dead face for what feels like forever before it moves slowly over the sleeping area highlighting a pile of empty blister packs beside her head. Like a detective nodding at evidence, the light bobs once before it moves over to spear into my eyes then drops to the floor in front of me.

I'm trying to get my breathing under control and blink away the spots that have formed in my eyes from the bright light when I hear the voice of the next woman in the mattress line.

"Huh, looks like she killed herself."

Her tone is so bland that I gape at her in disbelief and stutter out, "Wha…what, what do we do?"

She drops the light even further so it's pointing down at her lap, backlighting her face and making her look like a ghoul when she shrugs.

"Nothing. Just leave her. Someone will come get her in the morning. Go back to bed."

With that, she flicks the light off and lays back down, rolling over so her back is to me. My heart is racing out of control as I crab walk on hands and knees to my mattress where I push as far into the corner as I can. I wrap my arms around my knees and rock back and forth. Everything here is wrong. I can't live here. I'm used to doing a lot on my own but this is too much. I can't do it. From the violence and despair to the dead body that no one cares about four feet away from me, I just can't handle this alone! I yank my blanket from the bed and ball it up to cram into my backpack and manage to get my flat pillow halfway in before zippering it up as much as I can. I stagger to my feet and push my back against the pallets to give myself as much distance as possible from the body and slide past.

The woman with the flashlight must hear me because she rolls back over and mumbles, "Where are you going?"

I'm still having a hard time breathing right so it comes out breathless.

"Away…away from here…I can't stay here anymore."

She rolls back over with a barely audible, "Good luck, kid."

I slide the rest of the way past the last two mattresses where neither woman even stirs and bolt for the door that leads to the stairway between levels. I'll go up. I'll go up to the General and Jackson. I'll tell them what's happening down here and beg them to let me stay up with them. I hit the push bar on the door with all the force in my small body and it flies open and slams into the wall behind it. The only thought in my mind is to get to Jackson but it only takes me two steps up to hear the scuffle coming from the next landing. The sounds of fists hitting flesh and men cursing have me spinning on my toe and throwing myself in the opposite direction. Down and down I go passing the doors to the next level. I need to get away from the noises of pain and misery. I go until there is no more stairs, just a door that I push open and plunge through. My feet slide to a stop and I let the silence wash over me. This is what I need, no people and no ugly noises.

I stand there clutching my pack to my heaving chest as I look around. The train is still in the same place it was when we got off of it two weeks ago but there's no one here. I look around the platform and my eyes zero in on the familiar restroom signs, one for women and one for men. I hold my breath as I turn the handle for the ladies' room and crack the door. It's a single stall room that lights up with the door's motion. I blow out a pent-up breath in relief that it's completely empty and rush in to take care of business.

As I wash my hands with soap and warm water, I study the stranger in the mirror. I don't recognize this gaunt, haunted waif with dark circles under her eyes. The black curls are a matted, oily mess from not having a shower in weeks. I don't know who this girl is any more so I turn away and leave the room. I check to make sure the men's room is also empty before walking the length of the platform. It's completely empty except for a janitor's closet with cleaning supplies and soap refills for the restrooms. There's nothing else to see down here except the train so I walk up to one set of doors and stumble back when they automatically open. There's nothing in the train except for padded seats so I take one more look around the platform and then step onto the train. I pick a random seat and slide into it before pulling my pillow and blanket out of my pack. With the pillow between me and the glass of a window, I tug my blanket up to my chin and close my eyes. I listen to the silence all around me and feel safe for the first time in weeks. I don't want to leave here so I don't.

....

For the first day, I just sit and enjoy the peaceful solitude. I know it won't last and someone will come for me when they realize that the babysitter the General assigned me to is dead so I want to enjoy the quiet while I can. I take advantage of having a restroom all to myself by washing my hair and body with the hand soap using my blanket to dry off with. I hang it over a few seats to dry and eat the single ration that I've been keeping in my pack as a holdback. By the time night rolls around again I'm feeling more like myself and can analyze what I think is happening to the soldiers, who are really just people in uniforms. This is a transition for them. They have to deal with the loss of everything and everyone they loved and accept that they will be forced to live here for many years to come. It's like being sent to prison and I know a little bit about how that feels from being in orphanages and foster homes. You have no control over anything and it can drive a person a little bit mad. Add in lack of leadership and you get what's happening up there.

All I really know is that I want no part of it and I need to keep far away from them until they get a handle on the situation. I go to sleep for my second night on the train with the decision to stay here until someone comes looking for me. That means I need some supplies so tomorrow will be a busy day.

The first thing I do when I wake up is pull my tablet from my bag. I haven't looked at it since I left Jackson in his dad's quarters. I was too afraid that someone would take it from me so I kept it hidden in my backpack. When I turn it on and see it has a forty-seven percent charge on the battery, I make a note to look for electrical outlets so I can charge it up. I don't know if there are speakers down here so I open the message app and ask AIRIA. When her voice comes from the ceiling, I get my answer.

"Joslin Frost, how may I be of service?"

A grin of relief crosses my face. I had no way of knowing if the General had taken my clearance away or not but clearly, he has forgotten all about giving it to me in the first place so… Yay me! I have a few questions I need answered before I move forward with my plan so I just ask them.

"AIRIA, when was the last time anyone was on this level?"

"Joslin Frost, there has not been anyone on this level since the day of arrival."

Perfect, next question. "Is it possible to lock the stairwell door?"

"Joslin Frost, the stairwell door is equipped with a locking mechanism but only a green level clearance is able to engage it."

Darn it! No matter, I'm sure I can come up with some kind of door blocker or wedge that will at least give me some notice if someone tries to come in. Thinking of someone trying to come in…

"AIRIA, is there any way to know if someone is looking for me?"

"Joslin Frost, no one has requested your current location since you have entered the facility."

I chew on my lip in consideration before asking, "Is it possible for you to let me know if someone does ask about my whereabouts?"

"Joslin Frost, request logged."

Alright then. Now I'll know if someone's going to come looking for me. Until that happens I'm claiming this as my new home. I look around the train car and then get down on the floor to look at how the seats are attached to the floor of the car. Satisfied, I get back up and open a folder on the tablet that has all the supply locations and inventory lists in it. I'm going to need some things.

I'm nervous about going back on the higher levels but I know that when the soldiers are scheduled for training sessions in the central cleared area, I can move around without being seen. I'll have to be sneaky and it will take quite a lot of trips up and down the stairs to bring down all that I will need to live comfortably here but it will be so worth it to have peace and safety. I start tabbing through the screens, wishing I had a printer so I could have physical copies to make it easier, but I don't so I rummage through my pack and pull out the few school books I had with me the day the bombs dropped. I find a math workbook and a lined notebook and pencil so I start writing out what I need to get in priority and where to find each thing.

My stomach chooses that moment to start rumbling, reminding me that I've only had one meal in the past two days. Food goes on the top of the list. It's the number one priority and I start looking to see where the pallets of MRE's are stored. The idea of going to the food service area three times a day to get my food fills me with dread. I think it's best that if no one's looking for me I disappear so that anyone who's had contact with me in the last two weeks simply forgets that I exist. Second on the list will be bedding. I need somewhere better to sleep because trying to get a restful night sleep on these benches, even if they are padded, is going to get old pretty fast. Thankfully, the mattresses in stock are fairly thin and easy to roll up otherwise I wouldn't be able to haul one down the stairs without notice. After that, tools. I'm going to need to make some space in this train car to make it comfortable. I know my skinny arms aren't going to be able to undo the bolts holding the seats to the floor but I know all about leverage from my last science unit and I should be able to get them off with some type of crowbar and wrench. At least I can try anyway. I leave my list at those three things for now because they're the most important to me. I can always add to it later if I think of more things. Right now, I want food even if it is the bland rations we've been consuming for the past two weeks.

I dump everything out of my backpack and fling it over my shoulder. Without anything in it, it barely weighs more than a pound or two. I tuck my most important possession, my tablet, underneath one of the seats in case anyone comes down here while I'm gone. If they discover the stuff I'm leaving behind, at least I might be able to come back for it. I stand before the stairwell doorway with my hand halfway towards the push bar and pause. I have to talk myself into doing this even though I need the supplies from the higher levels. After what I saw last night I'm terrified of going back up.

I take a few deep breaths and finally force my feet to move. I let the door swing shut behind me and listen to the stairwell. It's quiet with none of the noise from the fight I heard last night so I slowly creep up, step by step. When I reach the door to the level that I had been staying in I have to take another few deep breaths to shore up my courage.

When I step through, I hear the sounds of the drill sergeants calling out instructions to the soldiers and breathe a sigh of relief. The majority of them will be in the center area and I should have a free path around the edges to get to the pallets where the boxes of MRE's are stored. After a few steps onto the level, I imagine I'm a ghost and I move smoothly from container to pallet without making any noise. I only stumble once and it's when I come to the area that used to be my home for the past two weeks.

I can't help my eyes tracking down the length of the mattresses expecting to see Captain Cote lying dead on her mattress still. I will my body to move when I see that all four of the mattresses are empty except for blankets and the one that I used to occupy has been removed. I shake my head to get the memory of her dead eyes out of it and turn away to complete my mission.

It's only a few more steps to where the pallets with the rations are located and I hunker down behind one of them and squint my eyes in the dimness to read the words stamped on the outside of the boxes through the shrink wrap that holds them stable on the pallet. A slight grin crosses my face when I read the words I had hoped to see. The next step is going to be getting through the shrink wrap without destroying all the stability of the stack. It takes a lot of work and my nails ache from tearing at the many levels of the plastic wrap, but I manage to make a big enough hole halfway up, in the center of the stack. Carefully, I slide out one of the cases, peel back the tape holding the flaps of the case closed and quickly start transferring the individual MRE's into my backpack until it can't fit anymore. I close the flaps of the mostly emptied case back up and try and get the little bit of stickiness left on the tape to keep it sealed and then push it back into the hole that I had pulled it from in the middle of the stack.

Happy with how my mission has gone so far, I try and quickly throw my pack back on to my back and stagger at the weight of it. I hunch my shoulders against the weight of all the meals and briefly consider leaving some of them behind for my next trip but decided that I need to toughen up and instead start shuffling back the way I came. I'm definitely not as smooth and ghost-like as I was on my way here but I make it back to the stairwell door without alerting anyone. I'm careful to check the stairwell to make sure it's empty before I enter it and guide the door closed so that it won't slam and alert anyone who might be on one of the other levels.

When I make it back to the train platform I let my pack drop off my shoulders and drag it the rest of the way into the train and throw myself down on one of the padded seats. A giddy laugh escapes me as the adrenaline that was rushing through my body floods away, leaving me exhausted. Using my foot, I drag my pack closer and dump the meals out on the floor. The giddy laugh turns to a groan.

The eight rations that I managed to cram into my pack isn't going to last me for very long. If I want to stock up enough food to last me for a while so I don't have to take the chance of continuing my sneaking missions, I'm going to have to carry more at a time. I stretch out my sore fingers and press on my aching nails before snatching up the closest ration and opening it for my first meal of the day. Before I go for my next load I need to get some calories into me. I have a feeling I'm going to need all the strength I can manage to stock up on enough food. As I eat my spaghetti and meatballs, I recalculate the small list that I had created for myself and realize that it's going to take days if not a week or more to get everything that I want to set up my new home.

Eleven days. It takes me eleven days to scavenge and steal all the supplies I need to set up what I'm now calling my nest. I have three hundred ration packs so that will last me at least a month before I need to go for more. I have two mattresses that I've stacked one on top of the other to create a cozy bed and multiple blankets that I snuggle into every night as well as three pillows that are so flat that stacked one on top of each other they make up a regular pillow.

I managed to find pallets that had the military's uniforms and found the smallest size that they come in, so I've now created a wardrobe consisting of hacked off pant legs and shirts that I have to roll the cuffs of the sleeves up five times to fit my small frame.

I covered the windows facing the platform with blankets to give myself a better sense of privacy in the car that I've made my home in. I left the ones on the other side uncovered because they face the rock wall of the tunnel. I know this train will never be used again because the only destination on the other end of the track is now a radioactive crater so I went to work tearing the car apart. I watched video tutorials from AIRIA's data banks to show me the proper way to apply leverage with a pry bar to a wrench to get the bolts started and then it was quick work to unscrew them from the floor of the car. Moving them out of the way out onto the platform was much harder. My final project was to locate a shower head fixture and hose. Once again, watching a video tutorial I taught myself how to create a showering system in the men's restroom.

At first, I worried constantly that someone would notice all the things that I had taken, but after taking another look at the inventory lists and comparing it to what I had stolen, I realized that I had barely scratched the surface of the supplies the military had stocked the bunker with. It was exhausting work and every night I would fall asleep with aching muscles but also content in the knowledge that I was finally in control of my life. No one was telling me what to do or where to go or what I could or couldn't do or even worse, ignoring me like I didn't exist. I could do anything I wanted down here. The only thing I truly feared was someone noticing that I was gone from the levels, finding me and forcing me back into that hellish life.

Once my projects were all completed and I had my nest just the way I wanted it, I found myself itching for another project. I considered spending my time watching the movies and TV shows that AIRIA has in her data banks but just the thought of watching what life used to be made my chest hurt with the knowledge that it was all gone and it would never be the same again. Looking for something to occupy my time I notice my math workbook sitting underneath a stack of uniforms and pull it out. I start flipping through it and before I realize what I was doing, I had found a pencil and started answering the questions. Unit after unit are completed until I come to the last page and close the book. It felt good to stretch my brain and I looked around for something else to do. I don't know how many years we're going to be stuck down here but I know I'm going to need knowledge to survive once the doors open, so I set up a schedule of grade-appropriate work in all the core subjects with AIRIA as my teacher.

I lose myself in learning and start moving quickly through the grade levels. With nothing else to occupy my time, there is nothing to do but learn. The only extracurricular subject I had any interest in was computer programming. I felt like I needed to honor my adopted parents by continuing to learn the subject they were most passionate about. I know AIRIA doesn't have feelings but she seems like an eager teacher to me, always willing to help me move my knowledge and learning forward.

When I had gone as far as I could with the limitations of my tablet, she sent me on another ghost mission to find a computer that would allow me to progress in learning programming. The model in storage she recommended would have been awesome but there was no way I could carry the heavy desktop monitor and tower without using some kind of help. That was just asking to get caught and I wasn't willing to chance it, so I had to settle for a less powerful laptop. My mind was a sponge, letting me learn everything I needed to know about code, backdoors, and viruses. She helped me learn by creating programs for me to fiddle with and simulations to learn how to combat viruses in codes and how to create them. She taught me everything I needed to know but would not allow me any access to her own programming code because of my yellow clearance level. Smart computer!

Four Years Ago...Joslin

I'm making my way through my final calculus unit when AIRIA interrupts me.

"Joslin Frost, General Mallor has inquired about your current location."

My whole body freezes and my pencil drops from my nerveless fingers to the floor and rolls away. Three years, it's been three years since I left the levels and not one person has given me or my location a second thought. Why now? What's happened that triggered his memory of me? I have to clear the fear and uncertainty from my throat to get my voice to work.

"AIRIA? Can you replay the conversation to me?"

"Joslin Frost, replaying audio."

"Sir! AIRIA has reported a development in the West bunker. Daniel Ross is no longer registering life signs. AIRIA has listed him as deceased and increased his daughter, Skylar's clearance to green."

There's a pause in the audio long enough that I'm getting ready to ask AIRIA a question when the voice of the General comes through the speakers.

"That's...unfortunate. It also complicates things. I had counted on Daniel being there to set up what we will need on our arrival. The last time I saw Skylar she was just a small child. I am uncertain how she will react when we arrive. It's a complication and I don't like complications."

"Sir, we could lower her clearance back to yellow so she wouldn't have access to AIRIA's higher functions. It would also keep her and the boy contained to the Ross' quarters."

"No, that would tip our hand. I think it's best if Miss Ross remains in the dark about our presence in her life. Leave her access at green but modify it so she has no access to the bunker's military defenses, more sensitive equipment,

and the power plant level. We wouldn't want her to get curious and stumble onto anything we will need as she ages. Most importantly, we will need to step up on monitoring her."

"Sir? You want me to watch her feeds continuously? A thirteen-year-old girl?"

If I wasn't so worried, I would laugh at the incredulous tone the soldier asked that in. I'm also extremely curious about what this west bunker is and about the girl, who is the same age as me.

"Yes, Johnson. I'm aware that it will be tedious but none of us has any experience with the nature of young...girls? AIRIA, what is the current location of Captain Cote? I believe I assigned her to mentor the young female that arrived with my son. Her name is...Jackeline...Jossie...JOSLIN! Joslin...last name unknown."

I start cursing. There it is! Some girl in another bunker rang the bell in the General's memory and I'm about to pay for it!

"General Mallor, Captain Cote is listed as deceased."

"What? When and how did that happen?"

"General Mallor, Captain Cote's death was recorded fourteen days after her arrival in the bunker. Cause of death is listed as suicide by overdose."

"That was over three years ago! Who's been taking care of the girl all this time and why wasn't I notified? Someone get me Donnelly!"

"General Mallor, Joslin - last name – Frost, has been monitored by me for the last three years. No personnel status update was requested for her."

"What do you mean, you've been monitoring her?"

"General Mallor, I have been tutoring Joslin Frost and advising her on all of her needs."

"How is that even possible? She doesn't even have the clearance to speak with you!"

"General Mallor, you assigned Joslin Frost a yellow clearance level on the day she arrived at the bunker. It was never rescinded."

I drop my head into my hands and try to hold back my tears. Not only will I lose my nest, he's going to take my clearance. After three years of having AIRIA as my only contact with the world, the loss of her will be like a hole in my body.

"Are you trying to tell me that there's been an unsupervised ten-year-old girl running around my bunker with a yellow clearance level for the past three years? Where exactly is Joslin Frost right now and what is she doing?"

"General Mallor, Joslin Frost has been under my supervision for the past three years and her current age is thirteen. Her current location is car D on the train level. She is currently working on a calculus equation."

"A what? Calculus? How can a thirteen-year-old girl understand that level of math?"

"General Mallor, Joslin Frost is nearing completion of her final grade of high school math. She has already completed the three other core subjects as well as chemistry, physics, and biology."

I chew on my lip in nervousness, waiting for his response but it's not aimed at AIRIA.

"Johnson, you have overwatch. I'm heading down into the levels to have a little chat with Miss Frost."

"Joslin Frost, end of audio replay."

I almost choke in fright at that. I push to my feet and look around frantically. I want to run and hide but I know that there's nowhere for me to go that AIRIA won't be able to find and direct him too. There's nothing I can do and I certainly don't want him to know that I just spied on him and know he's coming so I drop to the floor and fish my pencil out from under the seat. He could be here any minute so I should pretend I'm still working on my math. I lean over the paper that I was doing my equations on with my pencil poised but my hand is shaking so bad that I know it'll be a dead giveaway so I set my pencil down and tuck my hands under my thighs but stay leaned over like I'm still working on it. The equation I was working on blurs in front of my eyes and I feel like my skin is crawling with anticipation. I just want him to show up already and get this over with. There's nothing I can do to stop it from happening anyways.

The sound of the doors to the car automatically opening is almost a relief but the knot in my stomach is painful as I slowly lean back and turn my head to face him while trying to keep a tight hold on my emotions. I need to keep my reactions even because I have a feeling that this man will pounce on any sign of weakness. I keep my expression blank when my eyes meet his.

"Joslin Frost."

I'm proud that my voice is level when I respond. "General Mallor."

He steps into the car and my home and starts looking around with interest.

"It seems that I neglected to rescind your yellow clearance level when I sent you with Captain Cote."

I keep my mouth shut. Thanks to the audio replay from AIRIA, I know what he knows so I also know he's now fishing for a reaction from me so I wait him out.

"I was surprised to learn that you've been living in this train for the past three years. What made you choose this location and why didn't you inform me?"

The knot in my stomach starts to heat up with anger and I can't help but respond this time.

"I chose this place because it was the only area that wasn't crawling with unstable people! I was a ten-year-old girl afraid for my life and I didn't tell you because frankly, I didn't think you would care."

He raises an eyebrow at that and stands in front of me with his hands behind his back.

"Surely you exaggerate. There was a transition period for my personnel as they dealt with their new situation but you were never in any danger."

I shake my head at him in disbelief. "Really? How would you know? You weren't there when women were being beaten and raped or simply killing themselves. It was no place for a child!"

His face goes hard. "Be that as it may, you should have reported to me to let me know what your situation was."

I snort a humorous sarcastic laugh. "I did you a favor! I disappeared so that you wouldn't have to deal with me. We both know I wasn't supposed to be here and you had no desire to take care of me."

He nods in agreement, turns away from me and starts scanning the items I have on a makeshift table. I've used the cardboard cases of the MRE's to create bowls that are filled almost to the brim with the condiments, candy, gum, and matches that come in each ration pack. I've amassed quite the collection in the last three years but I couldn't bring myself to just throw them away. He uses a finger to stir each box's contents and then turns back to me.

"I'm not happy that you've spent the last three years stealing from me and destroying my property." He waves his hand at the changes I've made to alter the train car. "But, I was pleasantly surprised to learn from AIRIA that you chose to spend the rest of your time getting an education." I stay silent and wait. I know he's building up to something and it will most likely be my punishment.

"Tell me, Joslin, what other subjects have you studied besides the standard education?"

As he waits for my reply, I analyze the pros and cons of telling him about my computer skills. He makes the decision for me when he simply turns his eyes up to the speaker in the ceiling. All he needs to do is ask AIRIA and she'll tell him in detail just how proficient I am.

"Computer programing. I can read and write code." I spit out.

He lifts an eyebrow and claps his hands once. "Excellent! It's time for you to rejoin us. I have a job that is perfectly suited to you and your skills. I will assign a mentor to you and we will get you back where you belong."

He moves to turn away from me but the harsh "NO" I spit out has him turning back with a scowl.

"Excuse me?"

"You heard me. I'm not going back to that hell hole. Put me back into the levels and I'll be dead within a month. You might as well put me outside instead or just go ahead and kill me now."

He scoffs. "Are all teenage girls this dramatic? You will be perfectly safe back in the general population. Things have…stabilized in the last few years. I give you my word."

Now it's my turn to laugh mockingly. "Are you for real? Seriously, look at me! I'm thirteen and growing…" I wave up and down my body even as my cheeks heat in embarrassment.

Now's not the time to be vague about my concerns. "I would be a total target for some of your men. No way. If you force me back into the levels I promise you, I'll kill myself." At his dismissive expression, I growl, "That's a promise, not a threat, so go ahead and point me to the nearest exit!"

I can see his anger in the tense muscles of his jaw as he grits out, "What exactly do you want from me?"

I ignore the hope flaring in my chest and swing for the fences. "First, a job sounds great. I do have skills and I would like to contribute, but I'm not one of your soldiers and I won't become one. No forced training in fighting or guns, or at least not until I'm much older. Second, I keep my nest here and I get to lock the stairwell door for my safety." When he opens his mouth to argue, I quickly amend with, "To anyone without a green clearance, I mean! If I'm back in the levels where people will take notice of me, I don't want to risk anyone popping down here for an off the books visit. With that door open to anyone who wants to come down, I've been at risk the entire time I've been down here. It's only luck no one has stumbled upon me." At the slight incline of his head, I rush on. "Third and fourth, I get to continue my education, on my own time which means I'll need to keep my yellow clearance."

He stares at me like he's trying to break me but I just return his look without flinching.

"Fine! Anything else, your highness?"

The fact that he didn't deny me on any of it has me pushing the tiniest bit more.

"I don't need a mentor. AIRIA has been guiding me in all areas for the last three years and I haven't caused you any trouble so we can just stick to that. After all, my last mentor quit the job and life two weeks in. I'd rather not have to deal with another dead body. Besides, if you have a job for me than I'm sure that means I'll have a supervisor, right?"

He just shakes his head at me and twirls his finger before turning away. "Grab what you need for the day and follow me. Your job starts now."

I jump to my feet and pump my fist in victory behind his back before snatching up my tablet and following him out of the car. After three long years of being alone, I'm finally going back to the levels only this time not as a ghost and with some slight protection. I can only hope I'll survive it.

. . . .

I'm relieved when the General heads to the elevators instead of the stairs. At this time of day, the stairwell will be busy with soldiers moving from level to level to get to the different training areas. I had avoided the elevators on my ghost missions because you never know if someone would be in them. It does surprise me when he pokes the button for the top level, though.

I haven't made any inquiries to AIRIA about what was happening in the levels except for schedules because it didn't matter to me. I had assumed that the entire top level had been compromised and shut down after the evacuations. When the elevator doors open, I see that I was only half correct. The hallway that used to lead to the barracks double doors has been altered. The doors are not only sealed up but completely gone. The hallway ends in a blank wall of exposed dry-wall. They must have been able to contain the radiation to the barracks and front section of the bunker leaving the administrative offices and officer's quarters usable.

I followed the general as he takes us into the command center and stand just inside the doors, getting my first real look at where he runs things. One entire wall is covered in monitors with live feeds of the different levels and the exterior area of the bunker. My eyes move away quickly from them. I don't think I'd be able to control myself if I saw the dead bodies that are probably lying out there, nothing but skeletons now.

It took me two years to finally watch the footage of what happened outside that day to my family and the others that had tried to get into the bunker and it took over a year for my nightmares to stop being filled with those horrific images. Instead, I focus on the different feeds of the levels and shake my head in disbelief that I hadn't been caught on one of my many missions to scavenge supplies. When I look closely I see that most of the cameras are pointed towards where the soldiers have set up their beds, the food service areas and the training areas in the center of the levels. That makes my blood boil. Knowing that these people had a live feed of all the different abuses that were taking place during my brief time in the levels and did nothing to stop them. They could have done something. They could have stopped what was happening.

The general barks my name, breaking my gaze from the monitors and I swing my eyes to him.

"This is Captain Johnson, he will be your direct supervisor. Once we get you set up in your new position any questions or concerns that you have about what you're monitoring will be directed towards him."

Captain Johnson pushes away from his workstation to his feet and stares in disbelief between me and the general. "Sir? Her position?"

"That's correct. Miss Frost will be monitoring AIRIA West and the situation there."

Captain Johnson nods slowly but I can tell he's wondering why a girl my age would be put into any kind of position. He doesn't get an answer while I'm standing there as the General turns on his heel and waves me to follow him out of the control room. He leads me down the hallway with offices on either side until he comes to the one he wants and pushes the door open. He stands to the side and waves me through. It's a simple office with a computer and monitor and regular office tools sitting on an otherwise blank desk. I move around the desk and sit in the leather chair before looking up expectantly at him.

"This will be your office. I will have the feed directed to your monitor. There is a twin to this bunker in one of the western provinces that we need to keep tabs on. A good friend of mine had been taking care of it since the bombs dropped but I've recently learned that he has died, leaving his young daughter and son alone in the bunker. I need you to monitor her and make sure she doesn't get into anything that she shouldn't or damage the bunker in any way. It's extremely important for the facility to stay intact as when the skies clear and the radiation levels lower enough, we will be relocating to that area. That bunker and its supplies will be of the utmost importance in our efforts to start rebuilding. That's all you need to do. Watch her and notify Captain Johnson of any troubling activity that might occur."

I look from the blank monitor on the desk to him in confusion and say, "That's it? You basically want me to spy on another kid and make sure she doesn't break anything?"

He nods his head. "Yes, it's a fairly simple and straightforward job for you. We might possibly find some other duties for you in the future but for now, I believe you're the best person that we have for this position. After all, who better to understand the mindset of a thirteen-year-old girl but another one? I expect regular reports on her behavior and activities."

I'm not sure whether to complain about a stupid babysitting job or just be grateful for such easy work. Before I have a chance to respond, a voice I haven't heard for three years rings out from the hallway.

"Dad, there you are. I brought us lunch. Do you want to take it in the command center or in our quarters?"

My body freezes in place with warring emotions. Half of me is thrilled that I'm about to see my best friend for the first time after so long but the other half of me flushes in anger because if anyone should have been looking for me in the past three years it should have been him. The fact that Jackson never once asked AIRIA for my location or made any attempt to find me tells me that our friendship wasn't what I thought it was.

The general steps back further into the hall and motions with his head towards the open office door.

"Why don't you take those in there and share them. I'll get something for myself later." He spears me with a glance before disappearing from view only to be replaced a few seconds later by Jackson, holding two covered trays. His expression changes from mild interest to complete shock.

"Joss, Joslin? Oh my God! I can't believe it's you. Where have you been? I look for you every single time I'm on a lower level and I've never found you. Please tell me my dad didn't have you locked away somewhere?" His tone is joking but his eyes are dead serious like he really thinks his dad might have locked me away.

I lean back in the chair and crossed my arms, keeping my expression blank.

"I've been around. I'm surprised we haven't run into each other - considering we're locked inside a bunker with limited places to go. Maybe, you just didn't look hard enough. Then again you could have just asked AIRIA where I was if you really cared about where I've been for the past three years!"

His expression changes to surprise at the anger that fuels my voice during the last sentence and he shakes his head in denial.

"What are you talking about? I asked my dad every single day where you were. He always said that you were being taken care of. That I didn't need to have contact with you as

~ 141 ~

we were both doing our training. I missed you. I missed you so much! There's been so many times over the past three years that I would have given anything to talk to you."

I scoff at him. "Give me a break Jackson! We both know all you had to do was ask AIRIA and she would have told you where I was if you really wanted to see me."

His eyes flint up an annoyance. "Joslin, I don't have any clearance to talk to AIRIA. I don't know why you're mad at me but if I could have found you I would have."

I arch an eyebrow at him and turn my eyes to the ceiling. "AIRIA, what is Jackson Mallor's current clearance level?"

"Joslin Frost, Jackson Mallor is currently a yellow clearance."

The surprise on his face is so real that I find myself softening towards him. Maybe he really didn't know that he could still talk to AIRIA. I shake my head, it's going to be awhile before I can forgive him. He was the only person in this bunker on my side and I'm having a hard time knowing that he didn't fight for me. He finally steps into the room and sets the two trays he's holding down on the desk before settling into the chair across from me.

"Honestly Joss, I didn't know I could talk to her all this time. I'm so sorry. I would have come and found you if I knew. My dad, he's…he's just really difficult to deal with and he never says yes to me when I ask him for anything. After a while, I just gave up asking. I figured we find a way to run into each other eventually and we would make our own plans to meet up after that but I never saw you. Every time I went to the lower levels I looked and I never saw you anywhere. Where have you been?"

I look away from him as long-suppressed feelings flood through me. I've been without friends or any real human contact for so long that I feel tears pressing against the back of my eyes from his concern for me. I swallow back the tears and instead, lift the lid on the top tray to see what the smell that's driving me crazy is coming from. It's just a plain old meal of meat, potatoes and green beans but there's something glorious sitting on the tray beside the plate that I snatch up and hold to my nose. Bread, beautiful glorious bread. I've done a lot of things with the MRE's to make them more appealing but the same twelve meals over and over again for the last three years got real boring around two years and nine months ago. There's a lot of things that come in the ration packs but never bread, especially not freshly baked bread. There were times on my ghost missions that I would be able to smell them baking it and I would have to force my feet away from the food areas even as my mouth filled with saliva at the smell. Jackson's small laugh breaks the spell the fresh baked goodness has over me and my eyes move back to him.

"Geez Joss, it's like you've never seen bread before! What is going on with you?"

I glare at him and stuff half the slice into my mouth, quickly followed by the rest of it. I savor every bit of it and once I've swallowed it down I'm dying for more. I finally answer the question he's been asking.

"Well, if you really want to know, I've been hiding out all alone in one of the train cars for the past three years surviving off of stolen MRE's."

His jaw almost falls into his lap. His mouth is gaping at me in amazement and shock.

"What? I...uh...what?" He stutters out.

I pull the tray in front of me and start digging into the meal. It's plain food but it's not in a pouch so it might as well be a gourmet meal. When I've finished everything on the plate down to the last green bean, I lean back and study Jackson. Just like me, he's changed over the last few years. He's taller than the last time I saw him but so am I. Unlike my much longer hair, his has been almost shaved completely off.

There's just a light stubble of his once golden hair bristling on his scalp. He waited while I ate but I can tell he's almost vibrating to get an answer to his question so I give in.

"After the evacuation, that woman your dad sent me with, Captain Cote, she found us a spot on one of the lower levels and we stayed there for the first two weeks on the floor behind some pallets. Things down there were pretty bad with all the violence. So, long story short, after she killed herself, I ran away to the only place that didn't have any people, the level with the train that we came here in. I stole a bunch of supplies, made a nest and have been living there ever since. This morning your dad was reminded of me and came and found me. Other than AIRIA, he's the first person I've talked to in the last three years."

His face has gone through so many different emotional expressions at my short recap that I leave him to sort through them all and lift the lid on the second tray and slide out the slice of bread from under it. I eat this slice much slower as he begins his many questions.

"She killed herself? Oh…wow! That must have been horrible for you to see! I'm so sorry you had to go through that but what do you mean by all the violence down there? Did someone hurt or threaten you?"

I cock my head at him in consideration and realize he has no clue what I'm talking about.

"How long after the evacuations was it before you went down into the lower levels?"

He shrugs one shoulder. "I don't know, a couple of months, maybe. My dad had Donnelly set me up with some military school work to study. They kept my days filled with reading and learning strategy and military tactics. I didn't go down to start my physical training for at least two or three months after you left. I don't know exactly how long it was. Time sort of blurs here now."

I purse my lips. "So you really have no idea what was going on down there all that time?" He shakes his head so I blow a breath out.

"Well, let me tell you, I only managed to last two weeks before I ran for my life. There were so many fights going around where they would just beat on each other. The female soldiers were being abused and it didn't seem like there was any leadership whatsoever down there to keep anyone in check or put a stop to it and make things better, so I ran."

The expression on his face tells me he thinks I'm exaggerating and I don't have the energy to try and convince him so I simply ask AIRIA.

"AIRIA, how many deaths have been recorded since we entered the facilities?"

"Joslin Frost, one hundred and thirty-six personnel have been recorded as deceased since you entered the facilities."

I look at Jackson sadly. "Would you like me to get her to break that down into how many were murders versus how many were suicides?"

He shakes his head quickly. "No, no, I don't want to know that. I had no idea it was that bad! My dad has me kind of isolated up here and I only go down to the other levels for a few hours every day for training." His shoulders sag and defeat. "I can't believe that that's been going on all this time."

"Well, I imagine a lot of that happened in the beginning. Your dad probably got control after a few months or he wouldn't have risked sending you down there."

He nods unhappily and changes the subject. "So, you ran away and have been living in the train for all these years?" When I just nod, he asks, "What have you been doing the whole time then? It had to have gotten pretty boring with no one around to talk to."

I roll my eyes. "Tell me about it! It took me a couple of weeks to get my nest set up the way I wanted it to be but after that, there wasn't a whole lot for me to do so I just worked with AIRIA on school work. When your dad came and got me this morning I was wrapping up my last unit of grade twelve math. It's all I have left before I'm finished high school."

"Thirteen years old and graduated high school!" He says in awe. "You always were the best student in our class. It doesn't surprise me at all. So what are you going to be doing now that my dad has found you? And where are you going to be bunking?"

I glanced over at the monitor but it's still blank. "Well, he has a job for me where I'm supposed to be monitoring some kid in another bunker somewhere out west. I haven't started it yet so I don't know what it'll all entail but it sounds pretty boring to me. As for where I'm bunking, I'm staying put on the train. It's my home and I'm not willing to come back up here. I made a deal with your dad so that I can keep my clearance level to continue my education and stay down there in my home."

His expression turns to one full of glee. "Are you serious? Tell me! How did you manage to get my father to concede to anything?"

My voice is full of defiance when I tell him, "I simply told him that if he forced me into the levels again, well, that I would kill myself. I told him to point me to the nearest exit and let me go outside. I guess he didn't see those as options."

His voice changes to outraged disbelief. "Joslin! You wouldn't have actually done that, would you? I mean, kill yourself?"

I square up my shoulders. "I don't know what I would have done if he made me move back into the levels but it wouldn't have been pretty. I truly don't believe I would have made it if I had to go back there."

He reaches over the desk and takes my hand. "I'm just glad it didn't come to that. Does this mean that we'll be able to see each other now? Can I come down and visit you in your, what do you call it, nest?"

Before I have a chance to answer him the General's presence fills the open doorway. He glares at me before turning a sharp look to his son.

"Jackson are you not scheduled for a session at the shooting range right now? Just because your old friend has reappeared doesn't mean you get to shirk your duties."

Jackson jumps to his feet and sends an uncertain look my way so I turned to the General and ask, "Will Jackson be allowed to spend any time with me?"

The General's lips flatten an annoyance but he nods his head. "I suppose that would be acceptable, as long as it's outside of your working hours and you both agree to stay out of trouble."

We both eagerly not in agreement but I have to ask him, "Can you clear him to use the elevators and come down to my level? I just wanted to remind you that you did promise that the stairway and elevators will be locked to anyone below a green clearance, except for me and now Jackson." I keep the smile that wants to cross my face tucked away when he gives me a curt nod and then he points at the monitor in front of me.

"The West bunker's feeds have been rerouted to your monitor. If you're finished with your lunch break, get to work. Jackson on me!"

When his dad turns and leaves the doorway Jackson sends me a thumbs up and a small wave before darting out of the office to follow his father. I breathe out a sigh of relief. It looks like I not only got everything I want from the General but I've got my friend back too.

I turn to the monitor and press the power button to bring it to life. The screen splits into two feeds that show what looks like a normal interior of a home and a cavern that seems to have…is that a cow?

Last four years…Joslin

I spend my days watching over a girl and a boy far, far, away from me and slowly come to greatly admire her and fall in love with the little boy. After the first few months of watching them, I had gone back and watched the important moments of her journey inside the bunker. From the first day when she had to watch as her mother died and then later when she lost her father as well. I slowly find myself mimicking the things that she's doing in her bunker. I don't have animals to care for or a garden to tend to but what she's doing inspires me to realign my own education with these skills that will serve me well once I get out of this prison. I study crop rotation and how to garden as well as animal husbandry. When I learn all that I can about those subjects I move on to food harvesting and storage. I have an unlimited appetite for learning the skills that I'll need to not only survive but thrive in the future outside of this bunker. I stop seeing Skylar as someone that I have to babysit or spy on and instead start feeling friendship towards her and wishing that I could talk to her. The closest thing to that I can get is to share the things that she seems to enjoy. I start watching the TV shows and movies that she seems to enjoy and wish desperately that I can talk to her about some of the plot lines.

As I watch her practicing her kickboxing and martial arts skills as well as her practicing at the small shooting range she has, it makes me re-evaluate my own skills of survival. I basically have none. When I approached the General with the request to start training in some of these areas, it surprises him but he agrees that I should learn some of the skills that his soldiers are so proficient in. Jackson is thrilled to be my guide in those areas as he spent the last few years being trained while I was hiding out. I go about it the same way I did with my education, full on intensity and it's not long before I can match him whether it's shooting targets or taking him down to the mat in one-on-one sparring. He has height and weight on me but I learn all about pressure points and the other weaknesses in a human body and use them to my advantage. I create my own makeshift weights and, in the evenings while watching the shows that Skylar watches or learning homesteading skills, I make myself lift them until I end up with small bumps of muscles in my arms. I don't have the huge barracks that she has to run in but there is a small gym on the top level for the officers so on my lunch breaks I make use of the stationary bike and treadmill to strengthen my legs.

Over time, Jackson and I rebuild our friendship and he often joins me in the evenings down in the train to get some time away from his father. He vents his frustration and anger towards him to me in long curse-filled rants. I had brought up the subject of his mom and my parents showing up here but he was adamant that I was mistaken about who was outside. He bought his father's line about enemies trying to sabotage the bunker completely and feels a great hatred towards them for the damage they caused to the barracks. I decided then to keep the truth of that day to myself. Timing is everything and right now there's nothing to be gained by telling him the truth. We still have years before the doors will open and the status quo is working for me. So, I lend a sympathetic ear for his rants instead and encourage him to keep trying to forge a better relationship with his dad. I think it's important for Jackson to make his own decision on who his father is instead of me showing him, at least for now. One of my greatest strengths seems to be patience.

We've been in the bunker for five years when I start to notice that Jackson is looking more bruised than usual from his training sessions with the rest of the soldiers. When I asked him about it, it's clear how frustrated he is.

"I don't know what's going on! Everybody seems to be just pissed off all the time. It's like our training has shifted to nothing more than taking their frustrations out on each other. Honestly, I'm getting sick of it!"

I grimace in sympathy. "Well, what else is everyone doing down there besides training?"

He gives me a weird look. "What do you mean what else? There is nothing else! We get up, we eat, we shower, we train, we shoot and then we eat again. I don't know what they're doing in the evenings because I'm up here."

I shake my head but keep my thoughts to myself. I don't know how two teenage girls are smarter than grown men with military training but clearly, we are. The next day I go see the General in his office.

"Sir, do you have a moment to speak with me about something important?"

He doesn't bother looking up from the ledger that he's writing in just motions with his hand for me to speak.

"Sir, I'm hearing that morale is quite low down in the levels and I have a few suggestions to help rectify that."

He throws down his pencil, leans back in his chair and glares at me with a look full of disdain.

"Really, do tell how one teenage girl knows how to manage my men better than I do?"

I sit down in the seat facing his desk without an invitation and try to keep the smile from my face. As gruff as the general is in his manner, I think he enjoys our little verbal sparring sessions. I think the people he surrounds himself with tell him what they think he wants to hear instead of what he needs to hear. The fact that I don't really fear him and speak my mind must be refreshing for him.

"Sir, you've stated before that your plans, once we leave the bunker, will be to start rebuilding civilization, is that correct?" At his nod, I go on. "So how exactly are you and the people going to go about that? I know you plan for us to travel west to where the other bunker is and use the supplies in it but what exactly are you going to do with those supplies?" He narrows his eyes at me but doesn't respond so I push ahead. "Clearly all your soldiers know how to fight as that's what they've done in their training for the last five years but fighting skills are not the skills needed to rebuild anything. Do any of your people know anything about farming? The first step in rebuilding will be to clear the land and plant crops so I'm just wondering who's going to do that?"

The disdain has left his expression and it turns to curiosity as he leans forward and rests his elbows on the desk. "I have a few ideas in mind for that but let's hear your suggestions, Joslin."

"Sir, it's not just farming that they're going to need to know how to do. If we somehow manage to find livestock, people are going to need the skills to take care of them. Not only that, there isn't an indefinite amount of supplies in the western bunker. Eventually, things are going to start to run out. We will need people who know how to prepare food for storage such as drying and canning as well as homesteading skills like how to build and repair structures. People will need to know first aid and simple things like how to sew or knit. Also, how to hunt and prepare game, tan hides or tend bees. It goes on and on. If we plan on leaving the bunker within the next few years, you should implement a training program now that will teach them the skills to do all those things and more. Learning those skills goes directly towards your low morale problem as well."

He gives me a slow nod. "Explain."

"It's pretty simple actually. If you start setting them up in an education program to learn these skills it gives them something they very much need, hope. Right now, day after day, they do nothing but train. Train on how to fight, how to shoot their weapons and not much else. If you give them the education plan, it tells them that you believe we're going to get out of here and that they'll need these skills to one day get back to some form of normal life. Plain and simple, General, your people need hope that this isn't all their lives are going to be, inside this bunker with no future. Start training them on the skills they'll need to survive outside the bunker and they will all believe that they have a future and that in turn will see morale go up."

He swivels his chair away from me leans back and stares at the wall in silence. I know he's thinking by how his fingers are drumming against his desk blotter so I sit and wait. It takes him a good five minutes to sort through all he's thinking of before he finally turns back to me.

"These skills that they need to learn, AIRIA has all the material and information in her data banks?"

I nod my head. "She does, she has everything that they'll need."

"How do you know that?" He asks, not in sarcasm but with curiosity.

I try really hard not to roll my eyes or have any sarcasm in my own tone when I tell him, "Sir, I've been studying all those subjects for the past few years myself."

When he merely arches his eyebrows in surprise, I shrug. "Having a high school education and computer skills is great but neither one of those things will help me feed myself when the last MRE is gone."

"You not only surprise me, you impress me, Miss Frost." He then pays me what I'm sure in his mind is the ultimate compliment. "I'm glad I didn't go with my first reaction when I discovered you hiding on the bottom level and show you immediately to the nearest exit."

I don't bother replying to that as whatever I might say will come out soaked in venom.

"As you're familiar with the material, I'm putting you in charge of implementing the training program."

I shake my head at him. "Sorry, I can't do that."

"It wasn't a request, Joslin. Your current duties are light enough that you can set up alerts from AIRIA should anything occur in the western bunker that we need to know."

"Yes sir, I do have the time but I don't have the clearance level. I can pass the information on to someone with a green clearance so that they can put together the course material and schedule the different classes but I wouldn't have access to everything I would need to do that myself."

He considers me for a moment before asking a strange question. "Do you believe in doing what's best for the people in this bunker so that one day we can begin to rebuild outside and try and get back some of what we've lost?"

"Yes, sir."

"Do you believe that it will take each and every one of us working together to make that happen?"

"I do."

"Very well then, don't make me regret this. AIRIA, increase Joslin Frost's clearance level to green."

It takes all the will that I have in my body to hold it still and without expression as a fierce thrill courses through me. This man, this monster, that I despise more than anything has just handed me the keys not only to the kingdom but to my revenge.

Chapter Eleven...Present day, AIRIA WEST
Jackson

I poke at my eggs and the freshly sliced tomatoes on my plate with a scowl and then let out a deep sigh of frustration.

"Whatever is on your mind, just spit it out, Jackson." My father says.

I consider all the things that I want to say to him after the conversation I had with Joslin the day before but I know that she's right and nothing I say is going to sway him so I just shake my head and go back to poking at my breakfast with a muttered, "Are you ever going to let up?" It's hard to enjoy the fresh food knowing whose hard work had allowed us to have it, after the way my father had basically stolen all of it from Skylar.

"I do not have the time or the patience to deal with a moody teenager so whatever it is this time, get over it and get your head in the game." He says in a cold tone.

I lean back away from my plate and study him for a moment, looking for any signs of the understanding and caring dad I always hoped he would be but all I see is the General.

"It's not about me being moody, Dad. It's about our life, this life! I just want to know if you're ever going to let up on being so hardcore with everyone. I'm not talking about me, I'm used to that by now. I'm talking about all of it. Your soldiers, the people we picked up along the way, the survivors we found here, and Skylar. Why do you have to be so harsh with them all?"

He waves a dismissive hand. "I've explained this to you, Jackson. We only have a limited amount of time before the weather turns again. We know that the growing season will be shorter than before the bombs fell so we have to maximize our time before we are forced back inside again."

"Yeah, I get that Dad but I heard you when you interviewed that farmer that was working with Skylar and the others. She and her people had plans to do exactly what we're doing. They were about to start rebuilding as well, they just weren't going to be doing it with guns pointed at them."

He snorts contemptuously. "Oh, I'm sure they had grand plans to start rebuilding but without clear, concise leadership directing them on everything that needs to be done, they would only have gotten a fraction of the work in before it was too late."

I roll my eyes. "What you call leadership smells a lot like dictatorship, Dad."

"Oh, boo-hoo! So some feelings are going to get hurt and people are going to have to work harder than they want to. That's what it is going to take to truly start rebuilding everything that we have lost. Trust me, years down the road the history books will hail me as a hero and no one will care about a few hurt feelings or sore muscles."

"So we're back to just surviving then? We don't get to have any kind of life while we work to rebuild? You've basically got everyone not in uniform working like slaves and then what about these plans to repopulate? Sounds a lot like forced breeding to me!"

He studies me coldly for a moment before giving a small, annoyed shake of his head. "Is that what this is really about? You're worried about your friend Joslin? You know she's old enough and physically mature enough to have children, don't you?"

When I just glare at him he nods knowingly. "Jackson, you have to understand, growing crops is only part of the rebuilding process. So many lives were lost when the bombs fell and in the years after that our population was decimated. It's our duty to do everything we can to start increasing it in any way possible." He says it like I'm a small confused child.

I glare at him in disgust. "So that's it? Joslin, Skylar, and all the other women won't have any say in the matter? You're just going to pick out some men and say, go make them pregnant? Now you're not only a dictator but you're also a pimp?"

He cocks his head to one side, narrowing his eyes at me. "Why are you so sentimental about this girl? Joslin, I can understand because you have a history with her but what is it about Skylar that has you surging to her defense constantly? Seriously, you only met her once and that was when you were a very young child. Why do you care so much about what happens to her?"

I shove away from the table to get to my feet. "The better question would be, why don't you? Skylar's parents made you her godfather for a reason. Your only job in that role is to protect her! Was your friendship with her father all an act? It must have been considering the way you threw his children out of the only home they've had since the bombs dropped." I shake my head at him in disgusted disbelief. "Mom would be so disgusted by this right now!"

He gives a half-hearted shrug. "Of course, she would. You get your weakness from her. As sad as I am that your mother didn't make it, it's probably for the best. She wouldn't have done well in this new world. As for Daniel, Skylar's father, we were good friends but circumstances change and let's not forget that those two children wouldn't have even had this bunker if not for me. All in all, I'd say I provided enough for Daniel's children for the last seven years. It's better that the girl is out there with the other civilians. From what I've seen over the years on the video feeds, she's extremely strong-willed and would have ended up causing us many headaches down the road. Better that she knows her place from the start."

I fight back the furious tears I feel pressing against the back of my eyes at his casual dismissal of my mother's death and open my mouth to say something truly ugly but the door to the quarters opens at that moment, catching my attention.

My dad turns around and sees Joslin standing in the doorway and waves her in. "Joslin, good - do you have those figures that I wanted?" He asks her.

Joslin looks between me and my father with uncertainty before her expression goes carefully blank and she steps into the room. "Sir, everything is going as scheduled. We should have the secondary barracks and buildings completed at the growing fields in two days. Dr. Craven assures me that the civilians will be ready to resume their labor at that point."

He gives her a sharp nod. "Excellent! I want half the civilians relocated there as soon as the new buildings are complete. We've wasted enough time babying them and it's time for the real work to begin." He pushes away from the table and carries his empty plate into the kitchen and leaves it in the sink for me to clean up before spearing me with the look. "Jackson, I believe you have duties to attend to. I suggest you check your attitude and get to work." With those encouraging words, he strides out the door that Joslin had just come in, leaving her and I alone in Skylar's home.

I stare in anger at the empty door he's just gone through until it slides closed, furious at him and frustrated that there's nothing I can say or do to change the course of our future until Joslin breaks into my thoughts with her soft words.

"Jacks, are you okay?"

My eyes tear away from the door and soften when they meet hers. "Joss, you can't stay here. You were right about him. There's nothing that I can say or do to sway him from the path he's on and it's going to get uglier and uglier as time goes on. Tell me what I can do to help you? To help you prepare?"

She glances over her shoulder to make sure the door is closed before turning back to me with a frown. "If you really believe that then why aren't you coming with me? Don't you want to live a better life? Don't you want to live free of his control? Come with me, Jackson and help me rebuild the right way."

I lift my hands and scrub them hard over my face and into my hair, wanting to pull it out at the roots. "I want nothing more than to walk away and never have to see my father's arrogant, uncaring face again but I know he would never let me go." I drop my hands to my sides and shake my head in defeat. "Joss, please believe me when I say that I'd like nothing more than to go with you but the truth is, if I did go with you, your escape would be over before it even began. Think about it, he's not going to put a lot of manpower behind finding a few escapees. He might even just let you go your own way, but his only son? There's no way he'd let that stand. He wouldn't have a choice but to come after me with everything he's got. Not out of love or concern but to make a point to the rest of his men. He wouldn't have a choice but to make an example out of me. He probably wouldn't kill me but he'd make my life even more of a living hell than it is right now so just let that go and tell me what I can do to help right now."

She opens her mouth and I can tell by the expression on her face that she's about to start an argument for all the reasons why I should come anyways but then she surprises me when she slowly closes it and her face smooths out to a neutral expression. "We have two days. That's all we have to get as many supplies diverted to the summer camp as we can. Once the secondary barracks are set up, he plans to move half the civilian population down there permanently and then rotate the rest every few days. The people I want to go with me need to be here for this to work. Once they've been moved to the fields I won't have any way to get them out. So what I need from you is to go and get two of Skylar's friends to come and help you load up one of the trucks with as much as you can cram into it. I'm hoping you can make three trips today and two more tomorrow to give us the most supplies possible."

I nod my head and turn, grab my full plate and dump it in the sink. If my father wants it cleaned up he can get one of his lackeys to do it. "Consider it done," I tell her. "But don't you think someone's going to notice all these supplies being moved and not showing up at the fields?"

She sends me a smile of gratitude and shakes her head at the same time. "That won't be a problem. I'm in charge of the supply logistics. The only problem would be if someone saw you exiting the highway to go to the camp. It's very important that you keep an eye out on the highway and make sure none of our trucks are anywhere nearby when you exit the highway to head to the summer camp. As long as no one sees you, I'll take care of the rest on this end." She pauses to study my face carefully before giving me a sad frown. "I just want you to know that I want you with us. I know you feel you need to stay because he's the only family you have left but Jackson, sometimes family isn't in the blood. Sometimes family is in the heart and I consider you my family."

I step towards her, pull her into my arms and hug her tight. She's right, she is my family and I know that I probably wouldn't have been able to make it through the last four years without her by my side supporting me. I might not be able to go with her but I'm going to do everything in my power to give her the head start that she needs to survive.

Chapter Twelve...Rex

I sit on the side of my cot and take stock of my body and its various aches. I'm a little stiff and sore but nothing that won't loosen up once I start moving. I scratch at one of the hardened calluses on my palms and I'm thankful for all the wood chopping I had done over the years to harden my hands. All in all, after yesterday's brutal forced labor in the field I'm in not too bad shape.

I glance over at Skylar, who's sleeping peacefully with her bandaged hands tucked under her cheek and wince. She and Sasha are suffering the most out of all of us and I can only hope that when they decide to send us back to the fields they ease off a little bit. Better yet, we will find a way to get out of here before that even happens. Matty's giggle has me looking over to the side of the tent where he and Ben are sitting with Belle playing some kind of game. She looks up, catches my eyes and sends me a reassuring smile. Once again, I'm thankful for this woman who stepped into the role as Ben's mother.

Marsh comes over and settles on the cot beside me, offering up the crackers and cheese spread out of his morning ration but I shake my head. After the past few days of nothing but old MRE's, I'm ready to go back to eating the sprouts that had been one of our staple ingredients for so many years before moving into the bunker.

"So what do you want to do today, dude?"

I arch an eyebrow at him instead of responding when he leans back on his hands while looking around the crowded tent and shaking his head with a grin.

"Nothing? Well, I have a very busy schedule today! I have a nap scheduled in about twenty minutes and then there's lunch rations if they show up. Then after that, a very important second nap of the day." When I just shake my head at his sarcasm he groans. "I'm so bored! Not that I want to go back and dig in the dirt more but there's got to be something we could be doing to move our plan ahead, don't you think?"

I sigh with my own sense of frustration. "I wish. I'm so ready to get out of this place. All we can really do though is wait and see what that Joslin girl has planned. Skylar says she's got something in the works to get us out of here so all we can do is just sit around and wait until we get the signal to go."

Marsh nods in agreement but it's clear he's not happy with it and pushes to his feet. "Well then, maybe I'll move that first nap up to now instead of twenty minutes from now."

He's about to walk away when the flaps at the front of the tent open and we both turned to look and see the General's son, Jackson, step into the tent. He looks from cot to cot with uncertainty until he spots me and Marsh and then heads our way.

When he reaches us he glances down and catches sight of Skylar. His uncertain expression turns to one of pity. I don't like how he's looking at her considering it was his father that put her in this state so I snap my fingers to get his attention and ask, "Can I help you with something, man?"

He pulls his gaze away from Sky and looks back and forth between Marsh and I like he's considering something and then finally asks, "Uhh, how are you two feeling? I mean, after yesterday? Are you feeling okay?"

I know this is the man in charge's kid but his whole demeanor is nothing like his father's. He actually seems like he's not a bad guy so I keep my tone neutral to see what he's doing here.

"We're okay, better than the girls anyway. Just a little stiff and sore but nothing that moving around a little bit won't cure."

He nods his head. "Good, good, that's great. Um…do you think you would both be up to giving me a hand with a special project today?"

When we just stare at him blankly he glances around like he doesn't want anyone to overhear him.

"Um, it's for Joslin? She said you would be interested in giving me a hand with it?" He stammers out.

This perks both Marsh and I right up. If Joslin sent him that means it has to do with our escape and we're on board with anything he needs our help with. We both eagerly not our heads.

A look of relief flashes across his face. "Okay, um, then we should go and get started."

Marsh looks deeper into the tent until he sees his dad Lance, then points at himself and me before nodding his head in Jackson's direction. Lance looks the kid up and down before slowly nodding his head at Marsh to let him know he got the message. Belle must have been watching us because when I turn her way she gives a small wave and nod towards the boys to tell me she's got them.

We follow Jackson out of the tent and I'm surprised when he turns away from the main barracks doors and heads towards the smaller door in the rock wall that leads to Skylar's old home. He flips up the keypad cover punches in a code and then waves us to follow him into the airlock.

We're both standing behind him when he doesn't move to the next door but instead stops and addresses one of the speakers in the corner. "AIRIA, is there anyone in the living quarters right now?"

"Jackson Mallor, there is currently no one occupying the living quarters."

I see him chew on his lip while considering the reply before addressing AIRIA once again.

~ 163 ~

"Is there anyone in the cavern behind the living quarters or in the connecting tunnel to the barracks?"

"Jackson Mallor, both areas are currently empty of personnel."

I see the tension flow out of his shoulders as he palms open the door into Skylar's home and realize that whatever we're about to do, he doesn't want anyone to see. We follow him through the quarters and into the cavern where he keeps walking straight to the back garage area where Skylar's dad's truck used to be. Instead, there's a large cargo truck waiting there. He finally turns to us and pulls a piece of paper out of his pocket and holds it out to me.

"Uh, so Joslin has a list of things that she wants us to load on this truck. I don't know where a lot of it is but I'm sure AIRIA can tell us. Joslin says that everything on the list is on this side of the bunker so hopefully we won't have to worry about anyone else coming along and asking what we're doing."

I give the list he's handed me a quick scan before looking up at him and asking, "And what is it exactly that we're doing with it?"

He turns away from us like he doesn't want to answer the question and just shrugs one shoulder. "What we're doing is loading the truck with what's on the list. Let's start with that and we'll see how it goes from there."

Marsh and I exchange glances behind his back but this is the only game in town for us so we go along with what the guy wants and hopefully we'll get more answers as we go.

Thankfully, the truck has a retractable ramp to make things easier for loading because the first thing we have to put on it is two of Skylar's ATVs. Once those are on and secured in place with straps we start filling Jerry cans with gas from the internal pump on one side of the garage area. The list says twenty cans of fuel so I leave Marsh to start filling them up and head with Jackson to where the shipping crates are for the next items on the list. I'm happy we find a couple of dollies for us to use or we would have been hauling a lot of weight. Cases of MRE's, boxes filled with dried goods and foodstuffs are moved to the garage area and then loaded onto the truck. Hand-held farm equipment, gardening supplies as well as boxes of seeds and animal feed are checked off the list. It takes us just under two hours for the three of us to load the truck right to the brim with supplies. When Jackson pulls the overhead door down on the back of the truck and secures it, he turns and gave us a nervous look.

"Okay, so now we have to drive this stuff and then unload it at the other end."

Marsh looks at me and then turns back to Jackson. "Again, where exactly are we taking this stuff?"

Jackson looks nervously around like he's expecting someone to jump out at us any minute.

"Um, we're setting up a secondary site beside the fields you guys planted and all this stuff needs to go there."

Any charitable thoughts I had for the guy flee at those words. This had nothing to do with our escape. He just needed some labor to move more supplies for his people. Marsh and I exchange scowls before following Jackson around and climbing into the rear cab of the truck. I'm thinking maybe we can overpower the kid on the road and hold him hostage or something. See if we can make a deal to get the General to let our people go but I dismiss that idea when I see him move an assault rifle over between himself and the driver's door.

He hits a remote that is clipped to the visor, sending the overhead door in front of the truck up and the garage fills with early morning sunlight. Even though it's been a few days now that I've been out in the sun, it still gives me a thrill after so many years of clouds blanketing the sky.

We bump along the track that runs around the back and then beside the mountain wall the bunker is built into until we reach the front, where two soldiers stand blocking the way.

I can practically feel the tension rolling off Jackson and I can see a slight shaking of his hand when he reaches for the knob to roll down the window, making me wonder what's up with this guy. One of the guards takes a step closer to the truck and peers through the windshield. When his expression shows recognition of Jackson he steps back, says something to his partner and they wave us through. As soon as we've made it out of the cleared camp area Jackson blows out a huge breath like he's relieved and slumps back into his seat. He turns to us with a slight grin on his face.

"So, I'm sorry I couldn't tell you before but I don't trust the computer in the bunker. Who knows if my father has it monitoring everything I say. We haven't exactly been agreeing on most things lately so he could be keeping closer tabs on me." When Marsh and I just nod cautiously at him he continues. "Joslin found a place she wants you all to relocate to and these supplies are headed there. I know you guys don't have any reason to trust me but I'm taking a huge risk in helping all of you because of her. She doesn't deserve this life and I'm willing to go against my father to make sure she gets out of here."

A huge weight lifts off my shoulders at his words. I have about a thousand questions for him on how she's going to accomplish freeing us while under AIRIA's watchful eye, not to mention all the guards with guns. When I start to let loose with my question, he holds up a hand from the steering wheel in a stop gesture.

"All I can say is, I don't know. She hasn't shared what her plans are with me other than leaving here and taking you guys with her and it's probably better if I don't know how she plans to accomplish it. Trust me when I tell you, that girl is the smartest person I know." When we don't look very convinced, he says, "Really! She hid from my father for the first three years after the bombs dropped…in a bunker! Not only that, she managed to finish high school by age thirteen. In a bunker full of adult soldiers, she somehow managed to make herself indispensable to my dad, so trust me. If anyone can escape my father, it's her."

Marsh leans forward between the seats. "Dude, if you care so much for the girl why aren't you coming with us? I get that the big man is your dad but he seems like quite the hard-ass."

Jackson is silent for a few minutes as he concentrates on the road ahead of us and when he finally speaks it's in a quiet tone.

"He is a hard-ass and honestly sometimes I think he might even be evil. I can't come with you for two reasons. First, as much as I hate him sometimes, he's the only family I have left. And second, you guys have a better shot of him leaving you alone without me. There's no way he would let his only son run away. Not so much because he loves me because I'm not really sure that he does, but because it would make him look bad in front of his men."

Marsh leans back with a whispered, "Harsh!"

There's not much conversation after that as we move onto the main highway and the truck wheels eat up the miles. We're following the same route that the troop transports had driven us yesterday - towards where the fields are and we are almost there when Jackson slows the truck right down and stops in the middle of the road. He reaches into the glovebox, pulls out a pair of binoculars and hops out of the truck.

Marsh and I watch from the back seat as he scans the road in both directions before quickly jumping back into the truck, putting it in gear and flooring it up the exit ramp that we stopped beside. He keeps the pedal down and moves us quickly away from the highway until we enter a section covered in trees and then he slows us down to a safer speed.

Marsh and I are both leaning forward, eager to see where he's taking us but all I see ahead is more trees so I ask, "Where is this place we're headed to?"

He gives a snort of laughter. "Seeing is believing my friend! When she brought me here yesterday, I thought she was crazy but after looking around the location I think she's a genius. You'll see soon enough, it's not much further from here."

Twenty minutes later I see the first sign for a hotel resort ahead and can't help the groan that escapes me. If that's where Jackson's taking us we're going to have a problem. The last hotel we went to was traumatic, to say the least. He shoots me a quick look but doesn't comment on my groan or the sigh of relief that escapes me when we pass the entrance to the resort. Two miles later he finally turns off the road and what opens up in front of us when we leave the trees makes me laugh out loud.

Marsh must feel the same because he lets out a full-blown laugh. "Dude, we're going to Sleepaway Camp!"

Jackson drives the truck through the open log gates and pulls up in front of the biggest building. He turns to us in amusement. "Welcome to your new home, boys. I hope you like it because it's all you got to work with right now. Come on, let's get this stuff unloaded. Joslin wants us to do at least two more runs today."

We all exit the truck and I scan the camp in every direction, looking the buildings over but more importantly, the wall that surrounds it. I turn and look to Marsh and see the gleam in his eyes at what he sees too. This could work. This could work well. I have to hand it to that Joslin girl. For someone who spent the last seven years in a bunker, she really nailed it with this location for a new, defensible home. She is pretty smart. I have to wonder what else she has up her sleeve.

Chapter Thirteen...Skylar

I groggily open my eyes and have to blink them a few times to ease away the blur of sleep. They're not nearly as sore as they were when I laid down last night but they still feel puffy. The first thing I see is Ben and Matty on the cot across from me playing some kind of card game. I roll my head slightly to look around but there's no sign of Rex. What I do see is Lance sitting on the next cot over, leaned over with his elbows on his knees and his eyes fixed on the ground between his feet deep in thought. I try and push myself up into a sitting position, causing an involuntary moan to escape me at the ache in every single one of my muscles. I can't remember ever hurting like this in my whole life.

The noise alerts the two boys who send me grins. "Morning Skylar, you sure did sleep lots! It's almost lunchtime." Ben tells me.

I manage to get myself in a sitting position with my feet firmly on the floor and catch Lance's eyes when he looks up. He gives me a sympathetic grin and then turns and calls for Ethan. I follow his line of sight and see his partner further into the tent handing out pain pills like candy. Right now, I desperately want some of that candy for myself so I sigh with relief when he turns and heads my way.

"Skylar, how are you feeling? Sore? Achy?"

My mouth and throat are bone dry so I just nod my head wearily. Even that little bit of motion hurts and it feels like my neck is nothing but a thin stem holding up a very heavy bowling ball. He pats my shoulder and hands me three of the painkillers and a bottle of water that he brings out from underneath my cot.

"Your morning rations are under there too, Skylar. Just take it easy today give your body a chance to heal and rest."

As soon as I've downed the pills and half of the bottle of water I ask him, "What's going on? Are we not going to work today?"

"No, the doctor convinced the General that none of you would be able to make it through another day like yesterday so he's agreed that everyone out here in the tents will be given the next few days off for their bodies to heal and acclimatize to the work. The trucks did go out this morning but they were filled with soldiers, not our people."

I nod in relief and take another look around at all the people who are lounging on their cots or sitting on the floor leaning against them. I see a lot of familiar faces but two come up missing.

"Where's Rex and Marsh?" I ask him in concern.

His brow furrows in worry. "I really don't know where they went. The General's son, Jackson, came in first thing this morning and asked them if they were feeling up to helping him with a side project. They both agreed to go with him. I think they were hoping they'd be able to get some more information out of him or maybe build some kind of bond with him that might help us in the future. They've been gone for over four hours now and I'm starting to get a little worried."

I'd like to know where they went too but based on some of the things I learned from Joslin yesterday this might be to our benefit so I give him a reassuring smile. "I don't think you should worry Ethan. I've talked a little bit with Jackson and he seems like a pretty decent guy. He's not real happy with the way his father is running things so I don't think he'd do anything to put them in jeopardy."

I don't say anything else to him about what I've learned or what I hope the boys are up to. Joslin never said that Jackson was a part of her plans even if they always seem to be together. It's better to wait until they get back and we hear what they've been up to before I tell them all some of the things that Joslin had shared with me. Besides, there's way too many ears around us right now to keep anything on the down low.

Instead, I just thank him for the pain relievers and lay back down for twenty minutes to let them kick in before I attempt to move around again. Once the aches ease a bit, I roll off my cot and start doing some light stretching to try and get my muscles warmed up. My body's feeling slightly better but my hands are a lost cause, wrapped up in bandages the way they are. After making sure that Lance is going to watch over the boys I head to the flaps and ask the guard permission to use the restroom. He waves his hand at the flap so I slide out and take a look around. The cleared area inside the fence is quiet with not a lot of people around at this time of day. I look over and see that all the troop transport trucks are missing from where they line up to park and assume that the majority of the soldiers are out in the fields where we were working yesterday. I smirk to myself, let them enjoy a day of hard labor and see how they like it.

After I finish using the facilities of the temporary porta-potties, I'm about to head back to the tent when I hear a scuffle coming from around the corner. I only pause for a second before deciding it's not my business and take another step away when I hear the sound of flesh striking flesh and a cry that I recognize. I spin on my heel and take quick strides around the side of the porta-potties and see Sasha with her arm being gripped by one of the soldiers. From the red mark on her cheek, it's clear that he slapped her, I just don't know why - so I make it my business after all.

"What are you doing? Let go of her!" I snap at the man.

He barely glances my way before giving her arm another shake. "This is none of your concern. Go back to the tent!"

My tone is practically a growl when I say, "You're wrong! This is my business, she's a good friend of mine and I don't think she wants to be here with you any longer so why don't you just let her go and both of us will go back to the tent."

He turns to me with a furious scowl on his face and takes three menacing steps towards me, dragging Sasha along with him. I back up, matching the soldier step for step until we're back out into the opening in front of the porta-potties and in clear view of the tent. Even though I'm backing away from him as he's coming at me, his strides are longer than mine and he closes the gap quickly and raises his hand like he's about to slap me.

My hands are next to useless so I go to the other weapons that I have, kicking him in the shin as hard as I can with my heavy boot and when he leans over in pain, following up with my pointy elbow into his throat. I think he's more surprised that I dared to strike him than hurt because he quickly recovers and gives me a hard shove, causing me to fall on my butt. He had dropped Sasha's arm when I kicked him so now he has his hands free to draw his handgun and point it at me.

The soldiers guarding the tents must have seen me kicking and hitting their friend because two of them rush over towards us and unsling their rifles and point them in my direction. I slowly climb to my feet looking at all three of them in contempt while holding out my bandaged hands.

My voice is filled with scorn when I say, "Oh thank goodness you came to protect your friend with your big bad guns from the broken, damaged little girl! Shouldn't it be the other way around? Shouldn't you be protecting us girls from bad men like him? Is this why you enlisted in the military, so you can smack around young girls and then threaten them with weapons?"

I'm pleased to see one of the new arrivals immediately drop the barrel of his rifle to point at the ground and look away in shame but his partner just smirks and looks me up and down in a way that makes my skin crawl.

"Does it really matter why we enlisted before the apocalypse? That was then, this is now and in case you haven't noticed, now is when the strong survive and they do that by taking what they want when they want it. You might want to consider that in the future sweetheart, before you start attacking us. Trust me you won't like where it gets you. Now, why don't you go back to your tent and leave your friend here with us." He lets out a cold laugh. "Don't be jealous, I'm sure your turn will come soon enough."

An angry voice rings out and we all turn and see Jackson heading our way.

"Leave them alone, Matthias!"

I keep my relief to myself but it dries up pretty quick at the response of two of the soldiers. The one who had lowered his gun simply turns and walks back to the tents deciding not to stick around to see what's about to happen. But the one who threatened me does nothing but smirk and roll his eyes.

"What do you want, Jackson? This is none of your business."

Jackson finally reaches us and looks Sasha and me over in concern before turning to face the soldier called Matthias.

"I'm sure my father would disagree that it's not **his** business considering the girl you're threatening is his goddaughter."

A flash of uncertainty crosses Matthias' face before it falls back into a scowl.

"Really? Well if he was so concerned for her well-being, what is she doing out here instead of inside. I think we both know your father doesn't care what we do with these people as long as the crops get planted and then harvested."

Jackson feigns indifference. "Maybe my father doesn't care but you should keep in mind that Skylar's been living in this bunker for the last seven years with total control over AIRIA. AIRIA might be a computer but she's also an AI so she might have something to say about you causing harm to Skylar."

Right then, the voice of my long-term companion floods out from the communicator he has attached to his belt.

"Jackson Mallor and Skylar Ross, please take three steps to your left."

We immediately follow her instructions and move away but all eyes are pulled to the rock wall above the tents when we hear a mechanical noise coming from that direction. My jaw drops open in complete surprise when I see what looks like gun ports opening and massive rifle barrels slide out. The three huge barrels track around the area for a second before each one of them comes to rest pointing at Matthias. I want to giggle in glee for a split second when I think I've got my AIRIA back but when I follow Jackson's line of sight and see the girl, Joslin, standing there with a tablet in her hands speaking into it with Rex and Marsh standing behind her - I know I'm wrong. I realize AIRIA is not doing this to protect me but just following Joslin's orders. I look away from her back to the gun ports in disappointment and wish desperately to have control of AIRIA for just five minutes so I can ask her all the questions I have about external defenses and drones that I had no idea she had to deploy. But I know in my heart that I'll never speak to her again.

Matthias drops his rifle on to his sling and the soldier that was harassing Sasha quickly holsters his handgun. They start to back away but not without staring daggers at Jackson.

Matthias takes a parting shot at Jackson by saying, "Just keep in mind Jackson, we're not always going to be around where your pet robot can fight your battles for you.

Eventually, you're going to find yourself far away from your father and that computer, surrounded by real men doing real work and then we'll see what you're made of."

Jackson doesn't respond to the taunt, he just keeps his expression hard until they turn and walk away and then turns to Sasha and me with concern.

"Are you guys okay? Did they hurt you? Did we stop them in time?"

Sasha gushes her thanks to him but I just ignore him and look over his shoulder meeting Joslin's eyes with a hard look. This was lucky timing on their part to show up before something serious happened but it won't be long before they're not around when we really need them. Whatever she's planning it needs to happen and it needs to happen soon. As if she had read my mind, she gives me a sharp nod and mouths the word "soon" towards me before walking away. I look up at the rock wall and watch as the rifle barrels reverse back into their openings and the fake rock covers slide back over the holes like they were never there in the first place. I sigh and head back towards the tent where Rex and Marsh are waiting. As much as I want to know more about the guns and the plan, I know it's just two more things that I now have no control over.

Chapter Fourteen...Joslin

I rub my tired eyes as I scan through the lists on my tablet. I feel like I've been running since the minute we arrived here. After so many years of waiting to implement my plans, I'm slightly overwhelmed at the sheer amount of work that has needed to be done in the last few days to make all the dominoes fall perfectly. AIRIA was my lifeline in the east bunker and without the access I have to her none of this would be possible, but her voice is a constant drone in my ear as I try and monitor all the players in the game I'm playing, making me want to rip the wireless earpiece out of my ear and toss it across the room.

I lean back away from my desk and close my eyes to give them a rest as I mentally go through the checklist of all that I've done and what still needs to be done. The most important chess move I've made was completed within an hour of me entering this bunker for the first time when I uploaded the new coding I had created into AIRIA's core. Once that took effect, everything else was just logistics, lots of detailed logistics. Having Jackson on my side and willing to help let me achieve more than I thought I would be able to. With the three loads of supplies he managed to transport to the summer camp we will have a serious shot at not only surviving but even thriving there. With less than twenty-four hours to go before my plan engages, I'm hoping he'll be able to take two more loads minimum tomorrow before things step off.

I wearily open my eyes and turn my head to take in the rows of laptops, tablets and hard drives that I have set up on shelves across from my desk. They've been downloading content from AIRIA for the past three days and I estimate it will be complete by morning. I reach up and wrap one of my springy black curls around my index finger and give it a yank trying to get my brain back on track. There are so many things that I want to take from this place when I leave and I'm afraid they'll be so many things that I will forget. I give a soft sigh and lean back towards my tablet to go over my list one more time before I make the call to Skylar. All I can do is hope that I've pulled all the most important information and pray that I didn't miss something that will mean life or death down the road. I take a quick peek at the clock on the wall and see that I'm scheduled to make contact with Skylar in ten minutes. At this stage of the game, there's no way I could sit down and speak with her privately without someone being alerted to it so I had Jackson pass her a communicator along with a couple of earpieces so that we could have a private conversation. There are very important steps that need to be taken tomorrow evening when the plan kicks off and I need her and her people to be in certain places ready to do certain things.

The alarm I set for myself goes off when the ten minutes are up and I close out the files containing my lists. I glance at my door to reassure myself that it's still shut and locked.

"AIRIA, please monitor the hallway outside my office and alert me if anyone passes by. It's late so I'm not really worried about being overheard as most of the staff will be getting ready for lights out in the main barracks or officer quarters but now's not the time to get sloppy."

I had set the communicator Jackson gave to Skylar to vibrate to alert her and I can only hope she's smart enough to find a way to hide our communication. My earpiece comes alive with her whispered voice.

"This is Skylar and Lance is listening in as well."

That's good, a second set of ears to hear my instructions will hopefully make sure no mistakes are made.

"Skylar, Lance, please tell me that you're concealed right now and no one can overhear you speaking to me."

"Well, considering we're surrounded by at least fifty people, I'm doing the best I can." Her sarcastic whisper comes through just fine. "I'm lying on my cot with the blanket over my head and Lance is leaning against it on the floor. All the

~ 180 ~

people we trust are surrounding us so it's the best we can do to create a barrier between us and everyone else in the tent."

I bite my lip in worry but there's no other way to get this done and it's imperative that they play their part if this is going to work so I just launched into the instructions.

"Tomorrow evening, five minutes after your rations are delivered and the guards have cleared out I need you all ready to go. If all goes according to plan, the ten soldiers in the yard that will be guarding the tents and the gate will be disarmed and their weapons stacked in the center of the clearing. As soon as that's accomplished the communicator will vibrate once again and I will say the words, "Go now". If for some reason something goes wrong, I will say the word, "Abort". So far everything's on track and we should be good to go but better to be prepared for either outcome. If I say "Go now", I need you to gather everything you need from the tents including those bags you packed from your quarters, Skylar, and leave the tent - making your way to the door into your old quarters. You will not be returning to the tents so it's important to take everyone and everything that you want. As soon as you reach the door, AIRIA will let you in and you need to go into the back cavern. There will be an empty cargo truck parked in your garage area waiting for you as well as the livestock trailer. You need to get the cow and the chickens loaded as quickly as possible and the trailer hooked on to the truck. Besides that, you should strip your garden as much as possible. Bring the trays and pots and harvest what can't be moved. Go through the pantry and freezers and load as much as you can. You will have at most, twenty-five minutes to a half an hour to accomplish as much as you can before we will have to leave. I'm sure your friends have told you about the supplies that they took over in three runs today. They managed to accomplish a lot and tomorrow I'm hoping they'll be able to do two more runs but we were so far unable to touch any of the things that would alert the General. Other than the livestock, the most important thing you need to get is every weapon and bullet in your Armory. Those guns will be the only ones that we can take and they could make all the difference between us surviving on the outside and dying within the first few months. I will handle everything else on this side of things and meet you in the garage when it's time to go. There won't be a lot of time for questions at that point so anything you need to ask, do it now."

I wait for the flood of questions that I know is coming but instead all I get is silence. It goes on for so long that I'm about to ask if they received my instructions when Skylar's voice comes through again.

"Are we going to have to worry about them firing on us when we leave or chasing us?"

"No one will be coming after us and no one will be firing on us. I currently have complete control over AIRIA so she won't be a concern when we leave. The only thing you have to worry about is moving quickly out of the tents once I tell you to go and then gathering everything you can from the cavern and getting it loaded. I promise to answer all your questions once we've reached the summer camp and explain everything that's happened. I know it's a lot for me to ask you to trust me with, but I promise you I'm getting you out of here and I'm doing everything possible to make sure we've got a fighting chance in our new home."

A new voice comes through that I haven't heard before and I assume it's Lance.

"What about the rest of the people out here in the tents? Are they going to be left to deal with the fall out of this?" he asks.

I consider what to say to that and go for the brutal truth and hope they don't argue with me. "Everyone else outside will be free to leave. You should tell them to run once I give you the signal to go but not before then. It's imperative that we don't tip our hand so you must keep this just amongst yourselves until I say go. The only people I can guarantee safety to are the ones in your group. We may have an opportunity to recruit some of those people later on but for tomorrow night we have to just let them go and hope they can survive on their own. If you feel strongly about it, you could give a select few a rally point to meet at in a few days but keep in mind that if they are recaptured by any of the soldiers they may be forced to give up that information, putting us all at risk." I let out a sigh, wishing I could do more but knowing it's just not possible and continue. "I would love to say we could take everyone and help everyone out there but it's just not possible at this time, I'm sorry."

Lance's voice comes through. "We're in agreement. We'll look at saving the rest of the world later, right now, let's just save ourselves. We're on board with anything you need us to do Joslin and you have our gratitude. We will wait for your signal. Lance and Skylar, out."

I let the tension slide out of me for a few minutes as one more box gets checked on my list of things to do and let the one thing that I'm worried about the most flood back in, Jackson.

I don't know how he's going to react to what's going to happen tomorrow night. He deserves so much more then what his father has given him and I wish that he had chosen to come with us from the start. The only thing I can do is let this play out and pray that he comes with me in the end, even if our friendship is destroyed in the process. I push my tablet out of the way and lay my head on the desk for a few moments. I've barely slept since arriving here and the lack of sleep and stress are starting to catch up with me.

AIRIA's voice in my ear has me startling awake and I can tell from the sore stiffness in my back and neck that I've been sleeping in this position for a while. I blink a few times to clear the sleep from my eyes and look up at the clock to see that it's morning, early morning. It takes me a minute to process what AIRIA had said to me and I realized she was warning me that there were people in the hallway. I bring my tablet to life and tap in a quick command to end that notification and bring up a map that shows me the location of my main players in the bunker.

When I see Jackson and the General are still in Skylar's quarters I breathe out a sigh of relief. I jump to my feet and rush over to the shelves where all the download bars on every device are completed and start powering them down and stacking them in a crate that I have in the corner of my office. Once the last one is packed up I close the lid and have to heave it onto the small hand cart that I had brought in earlier yesterday. I take a minute to straighten my clothing and run my fingers through my messy hair before grabbing a clipboard from my desk as well as my tablet and wheeling the cart out the door. It's still quite early and there are not many people moving around yet. I only passed one sleepy soldier on my way to the doors to the tunnel that connect the bunker to Skylar's cavern.

I push the cart to the back of her cavern and leave it in the garage area, reminding myself to tell Jackson that it needs to go in one of the loads today and then head back towards the door to the living quarters. A quick glance at my watch shows me that I have a few minutes to kill before I can go in and see the General, so I stop at the animal pens and spend a minute looking them over.

The single cow in the pen makes its way over to me with its tail whooshing back and forth, almost like a dog's. It looks at me expectantly with its big round eyes and nods its head up and down like he's waiting for me to do something. I'm a little intimidated because I've never been around animals in my life but it seems friendly enough so I reach out and gently touch the soft spot between its eyes and give a small rub. I have to muffle the laugh that wants to burst out of me when it nods its head against my hand repeatedly like it wants me to rub harder. I kill time for a few minutes stroking the animal and wondering how it will feel once it's out in the sun able to walk freely over grass probably for the first time in its life. I know that Dr. Craven has inseminated it with some of the sperm stored in the clinic's coolers. Having a baby cow one day will be fun if it's as docile as this one. Standing there is very soothing and I find myself feeling more relaxed and confident in what's going to happen on this day. I give its head one last pat before turning and starting over to the door that goes into the living quarters and knocking.

The door slides open and I step through holding my tablet and clipboard as I've done every morning for the past few days to give the General an update on the current conditions of his troops and schedule.

The General is standing at the kitchen island drinking a cup of coffee. He nods his head at me and lifts his cup in salute.

"Good morning, Joslin. What do you have for me this morning?"

I return his nod and launched into my report. "Sir, no incidents to report outside or inside from last night. It seems like it was a quiet evening for everyone. The secondary barracks are on schedule with all the tents up, cots, bedding and rations in place. The latrines and storage buildings will be completed by the end of the day. We will be able to split and relocate the civilian workers as well as the troops to the secondary location tomorrow morning."

The General drains the last of his coffee and sets the cup in the sink before responding. "Excellent! We are on schedule and everything is going to plan."

"Yes sir, we are. Sir? Permission to speak freely?" He gives me his full attention with a nod of his head. "Sir, I'd like to speak to you about morale. It was a very long journey getting here and although the troops are happy with their new accommodations and better food, there are some rumblings about the pace that we are moving." When he just arches an eyebrow, I continue. "Sir, today is the last day that we will have all the soldiers in one place before moving a good portion of them down to the fields. I think this evening's meal would be the perfect opportunity to boost morale by holding a special dinner event to congratulate them on their hard work before we start on our next phase. I think it would go a long way towards their state of mind if you gave them this small reward and encouragement in what we're doing."

He looks at me shrewdly and taps his fingers against his chin. "Interesting. Jackson mentioned something similar yesterday about me never letting up. What do you suggest Miss Frost?"

"Sir, I suggest a special meal this evening once all of our people are back from the fields. I think it would do morale a world of good if you sat and ate with our people, engaging them in conversation. After dinner, I would suggest you give a motivational speech and then allow them to watch one of the many movies that AIRIA has in her database. There is a large retractable screen at one end of the barracks that we can lower. It's a small reward but one that I think would do a world of good before we get back to the hard work tomorrow." He studies me for a moment and then slowly nods his head in agreement.

"I think you're right Miss Frost. A little bit of a reward like that should boost everyone's spirits. Make it happen!"

"Yes sir, I will organize everything. Leave it to me, I'll make sure it will be a night to remember."

Chapter Fifteen...Skylar

Every minute of this day feels like an hour as it drags on and on. I spend most of the day trying to distract Ben and Matty to give Belle bit of a break from them, but my patience is paper thin. There are so many things that I don't know about this plan and what Joslin is planning to do that it's eating me alive inside and I can't keep my focus on the boys like I should. Rex finally takes pity on me and draws the two boys in with the continuation of a story he had started telling them about a galaxy far, far, away. I'm glad he stayed here today and let Lance take his place helping Marsh and Jackson with the supply runs. Lance wanted to get a feel for not only Jackson but also the location we will be going to as he will be in charge of most of our defenses once we get there. He also wanted to show Jackson where my dad's truck was hidden so that when we make our escape we can stop and pick it up along the way. Working vehicles aren't easy to come by and we can't afford to just leave it there to rust away or even worse - be found by someone else who can use it against us in the future.

There's a lot of things that I've had to let go control of since I opened the barracks to Rex and his people and even more once Uncle Bill showed up. As crazy in anticipation as I'm feeling today, I'm actually kind of surprised at myself by the way I'm handling the loss of control. I guess that means I've healed from the partly insane girl who used to live alone in a bunker with just a small boy. I'm still scared out of my mind for what might happen to Ben but putting my faith in others to watch out for him has eased the crazy that tends to live in my head some days. I look over at Belle, who's talking quietly with Sasha, and gnaw on one of my fingernails in concern.

I still think Sasha is a wild-card that could jeopardize everything if we're not careful but Belle has assured us that she's calmed down and fully on board with the plan. I think the hard day of labor they put us through and then being harassed by that soldier has finally made her realize that our only course of action is to escape this place. But no matter what Belle says, I'll be keeping my eye on her and making sure she doesn't do anything stupid that will ruin it for all of us.

By the time Lance and Marsh come back to the tent in the late afternoon, I've chewed off most of my fingernails to the quick. I want nothing more than to shoot to my feet and race towards them to find out all the details of what they learned today but there are too many eyes in this tent on me. I have to try really hard not to be filled with contempt towards all these people. The way they keep looking in my direction like I'm somehow going to save them all drives me crazy. Me, an almost eighteen-year-old girl is supposed to fix all their problems for them because I let them into the bunker at one point.

I can't believe that not one of them has stepped up to either fight, object, or plan something to get themselves out of this. I don't feel great about leaving them all here to face the fallout from our escape but at some point, people need to take some personal responsibility and do what needs to be done to survive on their own. I like Joslin's idea of trying to meet up with a few of them to bring them to the camp but from what I've seen of them so far over the last month or so, there's maybe five of them that would be good contributors to our group. Once we are away from here and safe, we will have to have a group meeting and decide who, if anyone, we should invite to join us.

Marsh heads over to join Rex and the boys but Lance comes down and sits on the cot across from me and leans over with his elbows on his knees.

"It's good Skylar. I couldn't have picked a better spot myself. There's a fort style log wall that goes all the way around the perimeter of the camp with multiple cabins and a central building that has a glass atrium. We'll be able to use it to grow plants in the winter if we can keep it heated well enough. There's a working well for water and a small stream that runs just outside the walls for more water. There's even enough open green space for us to put in a very large garden."

Some of the tension that's filled me today eases at his words but it doesn't completely go away.

"Do you truly believe we'll be able to survive there? I mean, who knows how long this season will last before the skies cloud up again and we get hit with winter. Will we be able to survive a winter there?"

He reaches across the narrow aisle and takes my hand and gives it a small squeeze before letting go.

"I wish I could give you a guarantee Skylar, but there are no guarantees anymore in this life. We can defend the place, there's good solid shelters to protect us from the elements and it's surrounded by forest so we won't run out of wood to burn to stay warm once the cold comes again. It's going to take a lot of work though, and we're going to need every single one of us going flat out to prepare for winter if we want to survive it. That being said, there are a lot of supplies there. I was extremely surprised to see just how much they managed to haul there yesterday and then with what we brought today, it's a lot. All I can tell you is that for the last seven years while we were out here, we had a lot less to work with and we managed to live."

Before I have a chance to ask him any more questions, Marsh throws himself down beside me on my cot causing me to bounce a few inches. "It's all good Skies! You need to have a little faith because the Jay's have got it going on. They totally hooked us up."

Deciphering some of the words that come out of Marsh's mouth is extremely entertaining for me but this time I have no clue. "The Jay's?"

He gives me his cocky grin and elbows me in my ribs with a bony elbow. "Yeah, you know, Jackson, Joslin…the Jay's? Seriously though, Dad is right. We're going to be living in the lap of luxury compared to what we had before you moved us into your digs." He lowers his voice and tilts his head closer to mine and whispers in awe, "TV's, man. She had us pack TV's!"

I stifle a laugh at his total kookiness and sigh instead. "Honestly Marsh, you got a good vibe from them? Do you think we can trust them?"

His expression turns serious as he slowly nods. "I can't really tell you my take on Joslin, cuz I haven't really chatted her up much but she is putting together a hell of a plan to get us out of here, so that's saying something. As for Jackson, he seems like a decent dude with a really, really, crappy ass-hat of a father. I feel kind of bad for him that he's not going to come with us. The blowback on this is going to be fierce and he's going to be feeling the pain from it for a while. Just take a deep breath and soldier on till go time, sister."

I lean my head against his shoulder and relax a bit. Marsh, Rex, and the others had survived for seven long years outside so I have to take their word on it. I tilt my head up towards him and grin. "Did you pack a generator to run those TV's?"

His face freezes in fear for a second before he shoves me away with a laugh. "Not one but two of them!"

And just like that, time speeds up. The flaps are pushed aside and in come the soldiers with the cases of MRE's and water bottles for our evening ration. My stomach is filled with rocks and my hands ache from clenching them. I had removed the bandages from them earlier in the day to let the air at the healing blisters so they would harden up. Painful or not, I need my hands-free for whatever might happen tonight. We wait for the first group of people to head to the front tables to collect their evening meal before pulling out the backpacks I had brought out with me when the General kicked me out of my quarters. Lance, Ethan and I are all armed with the handguns that I had brought out in the bags. We have them concealed underneath our untucked shirts. We don't know exactly what's about to go down but we want to be prepared for anything.

I count the seconds that turn into minutes as I wait for either the communicator to come to life in my hand or some kind of commotion from outside. Joslin had said that the guards in the cleared area would all be disarmed but I have no idea how she's going to accomplish that until my favorite voice rings out and the sound I had heard the day before when the gun ports slid back happens.

"Attention all armed military personnel, stack your weapons in the center of the clearing or you will be neutralized. All armed military personnel, disarm yourselves immediately and stack your weapons in the center of the clearing or you will be neutralized."

Marsh shoves to his feet and races to the front of the tent where he pulls back one of the flaps by a few inches and looks out. I hold my breath waiting for him to report back what he sees and try not to bark out the laugh that fills my chest when he turns to us with a huge grin. He rushes back to us and motions us to our feet.

"She's got red laser sight painting every single one of them! I think now would be a good time for us to move to the back of the tent."

We had all agreed that as much as we wanted to trust Joslin with getting us out of here, we would take precautions. We decided that going out the main flaps to the tent would paint too much of a tempting target on us so instead, we're using one of the sharp knives from my pack to cut a slit in the back corner of the tent closest to the doors of my former quarters. We're hoping with all the confusion outside will be able to slip out without being noticed and make it to our door when Joslin gives us the word to go.

At first, there's only fearful confusion coming from the other people in the tent but soon many of them are on their feet and rushing towards the front flaps to see what's happening outside. That helps clear the way for us to move to the back corner with only a few people giving us strange looks. I stand with the others in the back corner with the communicator clenched in my hand, willing it to come alive. Instead, AIRIA's voice rings out again from speakers that had been set up on the walls.

"Attention civilian population! You are now free to leave and you are encouraged to leave the area as quickly as possible. Do not approach the weapons or soldiers. I repeat do not approach the weapons or soldiers. Evacuate now! Evacuate now!"

She repeats the message one more time and then falls silent. It's all these scared people need to jump them into action. It only takes minutes for the tent to empty out and both Lance and Ethan are using the knives to cut a wide slit in the back of the canvas tent when the communicator in my hand finally comes alive with just two words.

"Go now."

I stuff the communicator in my pocket and grab tightly on to Ben's hand while Rex grabs Matty as we step through the opening and head straight for the door in the rock wall. All her exterior sensors must work now because the door slides open at our approach and I find a few of those rocks in my stomach start to unclench. The secondary door into the interior slides open as well and everyone starts filing through but I hang back for a moment and rush to one of the panels in the airlock and throw it open. I thrust my arm between the lines of hanging winter gear and scoop them off the hooks in one go, passing some of them to Benny so I can grab more. With my hands full, we hurry into our quarters and I dump them in the middle of the living room before dashing into the kitchen and grabbing a box of garbage bags. All the guys and Belle have gone through to the cavern but Sasha has hung back so I wave her forward and thrust some garbage bags into her arms.

"I need you and Benny to stuff as many of these jackets and snow pants as possible into the bags while I go back and grab boots."

I don't even wait for her to answer, just fly back into the airlock and start grabbing everything that I can and rushing it back into the living room to dump it onto the pile. I make four trips before I call it good and rush to stuff all the gear into bags as quickly as I can. It doesn't take the three of us long to get it done and thankfully Benny's strong enough to drag two of the bags on his own into the back cavern. I dumped my own bags in the center of it with his, grab Sasha and race the other way. Into the walk-in storage pantry with two carts we go. I'm happy to see Belle has beat us in there and she's pulling supplies off the shelves and loading her own cart as quick as her hands can move. Ben comes in after me and watches us for a few minutes with Matty at his side before calling to me,

"Sky, tell us what we can do to help. We can do stuff too!"

I don't even look at him as I'm too busy pulling the goods off and making sure they don't fall off the cart that I've piled high as I give him instructions.

"Go start stuffing chickens in cages, Benny. You know how to do it so show Maddie and get as many into cages as you can, even if they're a little bit squashed they'll be fine for a couple hours until we get where we're going." His little voice is filled with enthusiasm as he shouts out,

"We can do it! We won't let you down Sky!"

When our carts can't take one more item without the whole stack toppling, we push them out of the pantry and across the cavern over the bridge towards the garage, where we leave them. I rush over to the far left back corner of the cavern with the two girls right on my heels and grab stacks of empty bins and start passing them out to them. We need to get as many of the supplies that we have on our carts into these bins so we can load them onto the truck, otherwise we'll have food everywhere that will end up getting stepped on and destroyed. In a world where every calorie counts we can't screw this up with carelessness.

As soon as we've transferred all the supplies into the bins we leave them there for the boys to load and carry the rest of the empty bins on the carts back to the pantry for another run. I desperately want to look at my watch to see how much time has gone by but I'm terrified knowing that every second counts. As soon as we've cleared out the majority of the goods from the pantry, I head to the walk-in freezers. Belle and Sasha have been following me move for move so when I pull the door open, Belle reaches out and grabs my arm.

"Skylar, there's no point in taking any of that. We have no way to keep it frozen and it'll just spoil."

I pull my arm away from her and shake my head in disagreement. "No, we need to take as much of the meat as possible. We can cook all of it and turn it into jerky or can some of it. It could mean the difference between survival and death from starvation this winter. We have to take the time to grab as much as we can."

I rush in and start sweeping the frozen metal racks of everything on them into the bins and by the time we're out of room in the plastic bins, my arms and hands are frozen numb but I don't let it slow me down. We push the three carts back across the cavern and I take a look around to see how the boys are making out. The door to my Armory is wide open and I can see that every drawer and the glass doors that protected the weapons have been thrown open and are empty. The bins from the pantry that we had left for them are gone and Benny's small voice has me swinging around.

"Out of the way! Farmer Ben coming through!"

The tension and stress of the last few minutes is so overwhelming that my legs are shaking but the sight coming towards me has me bursting out in laughter. Ben has somehow got a rope around Nod's neck and he's leading her like she's a dog going for a walk. Following behind him is Rex and Marsh carrying cages of extremely agitated and irritated chickens. Me and the girls quickly move the carts out of their way as the barnyard progression goes past us and then we push our carts behind them to the garage. I only stick around for a minute to watch Ben calmly walking his pet up the ramp into the back of the livestock trailer with an amused shake of my head. The sight of him helping out with such confidence eases some of my fears and makes me feel like we might actually make it out of here in one piece.

I waive the girls to follow me and we head to the garden. We're only going to be able to take about sixty percent of the live plants that are in trays and pots. The rest are in built-in beds and there's no way we're going to have time to dismantle them and take them with us. I start viciously pulling out half grown carrots, onions, potatoes and anything else that looks close to being ripe. Once again, we fill our carts to overflowing and push them back to the garage for the boys to load before repeating the process two more times.

With the garden cleared out, there's only one last thing I feel we need. The girls follow me to a shipping container that my Dad had stocked full of toilet paper and feminine hygiene products. I stifle a giggle at Belle's and Sasha's expressions of pure joy when I swing the metal doors open and they see what's inside. Once the carts are loaded, I do let out the laugh that fills my throat when I see both of them stuffing their shirts with tampons but then do the same. I mean, come on! A girl can never have too many, right?

We're heading back for a fourth pass of anything we might have missed or anything else we can think to grab when Marsh goes racing past us giggling maniacally. In his hands, he's clutching Ben's Xbox with a stack of games on top of it that goes all the way up to under his chin. I just shake my head but I feel my own grin splitting my face. The feeling slides away when the double doors to the tunnel swing open and Joslin comes through, practically carrying Jackson, who's in very bad shape. I don't think I've ever seen anyone's face so pale before and the way she's holding him up I think he must be injured in some way. I turn my head and scream for Ethan to come help her as I rush towards her to give her a hand. Her face is grim but there's a fierce triumph shining from her eyes and she nods her head towards me.

"Time to go. We don't have much time!" The words have barely left her mouth when the lighting changes from the steady white fluorescence to a flashing red and AIRIA's voice plays out of every speaker in the cavern.

"Attention! Attention! All personnel must evacuate the facilities immediately. Self-destruct sequence initiated. This facility will self-destruct in five minutes."

The message repeats over and over as I stare at Joslin in complete shock. Images flash through my mind of every moment that I've spent inside this bunker. From the last moments that I had with my mother to finding my father dead outside and all the milestones that Ben crossed as he grew up. This is my home, this is my life, this is all I have left of my parents and she's killed it? She's killed it all. I finally find my voice and when it comes out it's in a roar.

"WHAT DID YOU DO?"

My furious expression and the roared question don't intimidate her in the least as her face stays firm and determined but her tone is defiant when she states,

"I did what I had to!"

Chapter Sixteen...Joslin

The stage is set as I watch the last of the players move into position. The final soldier returning from the fields comes in through the overhead door to the barracks and it closes behind him. A quick look at my tablet shows the only soldiers outside now are the ones guarding the tents and the gate to the fence. I open the command file that I've prepared for this moment and start tapping out commands. The first one I send is for all doors to be locked down except for the door leading into Skylar's quarters. The next one is for AIRIA to disarm the soldiers outside. I minimize the screen and walk out onto the barracks floor where the tables are filling up with soldiers who are enjoying their fine meal of steak, baked potatoes, and fresh vegetables. The steak might have been in the freezers here for a few years, but judging how the people are devouring it, it must still taste pretty good.

The General is mingling with his men, moving from table to table chatting them up, something I've hardly ever seen him do. Judging by the smiles he's receiving, it's going over well. I leave him to it and turn away to check on the next part of the evening while keeping an eye on the line of guards handing in their weapons and truck keys to the armory so they can go and get their own meals.

I head towards the front of the barracks to make sure that all the chairs have been set up in front of the huge screen that has been lowered from the ceiling. There were plenty of eager volunteers to move all the bunks tightly together at the far end once they learned they were going to get a movie night. It almost makes me sad how such a small reward has made them so happy. I shake the thought away and stride up to just under the screen where there's a microphone stand on a small portable platform. I check the wiring to make sure that it's plugged in and ready to go for when the General gives his motivational speech to his troops.

When AIRIA's voice comes through my earpiece telling me that the soldiers outside have been disarmed and civilians ordered to leave, I quickly look around to make sure I'm alone then tap a button on my tablet and say the words, "Go now". The tension inside of me has me feeling pulled tight but my expression is kept carefully neutral. The game is moving forward, now all I need is the will to not only finish, but to win it.

When I turn around, I see the line to the Armory only has two soldiers left so I head that way. By the time I reach it, both of the soldiers in line have handed in their rifles and are practically jogging to get to their dinner. I stop in the doorway and lean my head through, spotting Major Boucher, who's the head of supply. He eyes me with caution as I have no reason to be anywhere near the armory so I send him an innocent smile.

"Major Boucher, are you aware that they are serving steak and baked potatoes with all the fixings for dinner tonight? Why don't you join the rest of the men and enjoy a real meal for once?"

The caution leaves his face and turns to one of wistfulness instead. "Thank you, Miss Frost. I would love nothing more than to sink my teeth into a real piece of beef but I will have to wait for Captain Roy to come back from his dinner to relieve me."

I feign surprise. "Of course, you wouldn't want to leave the armory unmanned, which would be against regulations. But you could lock it down. I'm pretty sure no one's going to need any weapons in the next hour or so. That is unless the kitchen staff doesn't cook the steaks well enough. Someone might need a rifle to put their steak out of its misery if it's too rare!"

The Major perks up at that and laughs at my silly joke but shakes his head. "It's sweet of you to think of me Miss Frost but I wouldn't want to interrupt the General when he's having such a good time interacting with the troops right now, just to get him to authorize AIRIA to lockdown the armory."

I shoot my eyebrows up like I'm surprised and give a little laugh. "Oh! That is so considerate of you. He does seem like he's having a good time. It's nice to see the General relaxing and enjoying himself after so many years of hardship. But if it's just a matter of authorizing AIRIA to lock the Armory down, I can do that for you. Were you aware that I have a green clearance level?"

He looks at me with a touch of surprise. "Really? I did not know that you had a green level."

I step back from the doorway with a grin and wave him out. "Really, I do! Close the door and I'll authorize it while you're standing here so you can be sure that it's locked up tight and then you can go and enjoy yourself with the rest."

He sends me an uncertain look but pulls the door closed and looks at me expectantly like I'm trying to trick him.

"AIRIA, please lock down the barracks' armory."

"Joslin Frost, armory secure." She confirms.

I pat the Major on his arm and wave towards the food line. "Come and find me when you want me to open it again for you but in the meantime enjoy your meal and don't forget we're having a special movie screening tonight as well. You wouldn't want to miss it!"

He fires off a sloppy salute in gratitude before hustling across the barracks to get in line. I open my command file again and tap out the next command. Now the armory won't open for anyone but me. I walk around the perimeter of the barracks, taking it all in, and spot Jackson rising from one of the tables with a tray. I head in his direction as he passes his dirty dishes through one of the kitchen windows to the dishwashers. Before I get to him, the General crosses between us and comes to a stop in front of me.

"Miss Frost, there you are! I'd like to commend you for all you've done organizing this evening. It was sound advice that you gave me and clearly, by the response from the troops, it was something that needed to be done. You continually impress me for someone who is so young. You're incredibly mature and composed for someone of your age. Once we complete the first phase, I'd like to discuss increasing your duties in the future. You've become a real asset to me and our people."

I keep a pleasant smile on my face and the simple thank you I should say to him doesn't come out as planned. Instead, I speak from my heart.

"Sir, did you know I was adopted two years before the bombs fell? I had been in foster care or an orphanage for all of my life until they adopted me. It was the first chance I ever had to have a family of my own. To really, truly know what it meant to be loved."

He seems slightly confused by why I'm telling him this but he's in a good mood so he indulges me.

"I'm sorry, Miss Frost, I was unaware of that. But learning that makes me even more proud of all you've had to overcome to become such an asset to us all."

My smile grows larger. "Thank you, Sir. I like to think that everything I do now, I do to make them proud, to honor their memory. Take my computer skills for example. My adopted parents were programmers and taught me many things and gave me my love for all things computers. Yes, sir, I do what I do to honor them." He's starting to look slightly uncomfortable so I forge on. "Sir, forgive me, the reason I'm telling you this is I thought you might want to include something in your speech to the personnel tonight. Something along the lines of, even though we've lost our loved ones, they would be proud of what we're doing to try and rebuild. I think it would mean a lot to the people if you reminded them of everything we're working for."

He studies me with a blank expression long enough that I start to feel nauseous before he finally nods his head and a pleased smile crosses his face. "Another excellent idea, Miss Frost. I will remind them that their family, friends and loved ones would be proud of everything we're trying to accomplish here."

I see Jackson heading our way so I wrap it up. "Very good, Sir. I'm sure everything you say tonight will fill the troops with determination for what's to come. It looks like quite a few of them have relocated to the chairs where we'll be screening the movie if you want to head in that direction. We wouldn't want the evening to run too late with us having big plans for first thing in the morning."

He looks over his shoulder and sees the chairs filling with his people so he gives me a brief nod and turns on his heel. He passes his son without a word and heads towards where the microphone is set up. Jackson joins me with a frown on his face and mutters under his breath just loud enough for me to hear, "Like I don't even exist to him."

I let my hands slip into his and give it a squeeze before letting it go and lifting my tablet up to my chest. I can't bring myself to look at him when I say in a low voice, "I'm so sorry Jackson. I'm sorry."

He bumps his shoulder into mine in a friendly gesture but before he can say anything his father's voice comes over the microphone capturing his attention and letting me angle slightly away from him. I take a deep breath and my finger hovers over the command that I'm more than ready to give. The General is rambling about the hard journey across the country to get here and all the things we had to sacrifice during the long years of being in the bunker in the east. When he starts talking to them about their lost family, friends and loved ones and how we would be rebuilding the world in their memory, my finger stabs down on the command that brings the huge screen behind him and every other screen in the bunker to life. I made sure that we had extra monitors installed all the way around the bunker and even in the kitchen in the guise of making sure everyone had a chance to watch the rare entertainment of a movie. I wanted to be sure that not a single person would miss what I had to show them. The video playing behind the General is showing the faces of every single person that made it to the bunker the day the bombs fell. Right away, people start calling out, "My wife! My mother! Those are my kids!" - until there are so many voices calling out that you couldn't even make out individual words anymore.

I keep my eyes off of the screen, as every image is already embedded into my memory permanently and stay focused on the General's face as his expression turns to bewildered. He's nodding his head as the people yell out the names of their loved ones that they see on the screen behind him as if he thinks that they're saying their names to honor their memory. The soft gasp from Jackson lets me know he's seen his mother but I don't look his way. I keep my eyes on the General waiting for the moment when clarity will come to him but it doesn't come until his microphone cuts out and every speaker in the barracks blare's out with the words he uttered that horrible day seven years ago.

"Letting civilians into this bunker will only cause distraction and chaos to the soldiers. They'll need to stay focused and train until they're as sharp as a fine steel blade if we're to make it through the years ahead. They already believed that all those people are dead so we're going to keep it that way. We all must sacrifice for the greater good."

I watch the realization of what's coming cross his features and he frantically scans the crowd that is now on its feet. He manages to yell out, "SHUT…" before the sounds of multiple bullets firing drowns out the rest of his sentence. Anyone not on their feet by then surges up with yells, screams, and roars of agony and rage. As the crowd surges toward him in a murderous rage his eyes finally land on me and I see the moment he realizes that I'm the one who's done this to him.

I raise my hand up to my brow and send him a crisp salute before he's taken down by the first of his men to reach him. I stand and watch as arms and feet fly at him even though I can no longer see him and wait to feel the sense of triumph, the sense of justice, that I thought I would feel after all these years of holding the pain inside - but all I feel is hollow. When the sound of a single gunshot echoes out through the room followed by cheers from the crowd that was beating the General, the feeling I have inside is as if a door has closed.

I'm about to turn away to pull Jackson from the area when movement rushing towards me catches my eye and I spin around. Donnelly is pounding towards me with a look of murderous rage twisting his features into an ugly mask. He knows I did this. He's never liked me from the start and he's always been bitter that the General took me under his wing and raised my clearance level. He's made it halfway to me from across the barracks when one of the soldiers tackles him from the side, with a few others piling on top. They know that Donnelly is the General's right-hand man and all-around lackey. The General often used Donnelly to mete out punishment and many of them suffered under his cruel control. When it's clear there's no way he'll be getting back to his feet under so many bodies, I turn away and grab a hold of Jackson's arm.

His face is so pale as tears wash down his cheeks continuously. The sound coming from his throat is something you might hear from a wounded animal caught in a trap. There's so much pain, grief, and betrayal in it that it hurts every cell in my body to hear. I need to get him out of here.

He just watched his mother being gunned down and now his father is dead too. Even if at some point he comes out of his shock and his grief turns to hate towards me, I can't leave him here with these people. I don't know if they'll blame a teenager for his father's crimes but I'm not willing to take that chance, so I haul him as fast as I can out of the barracks and through the double doors to the administration hallway. He staggers against the wall like he's going to collapse but we're still not safe here so I use every ounce of strength in my body to haul him back onto his feet and drag him to the double doors that lead to the tunnel that'll get us into Skylar's area.

As soon as we clear the next set of doors and they close behind us, I shout out to AIRIA to lock it down and initiate program End Game. My hands are full just keeping Jackson up and moving to be able to use the tablet to send the commands but verbal commands work just as well and I no longer have any fear of anyone overhearing me.

End Game is a virus that I built into the code that I uploaded into AIRIA's core on the day we arrived and it takes four minutes to cycle through all her barriers. We've just managed to make it to the other end of the tunnel and through the cavern doors when the lights change to red and AIRIA announces the evacuation. Skylar is running towards me but she skids to a stop when she understands what the words that are coming from AIRIA's speakers mean. That the one person she always thought she could count on is about to die.

"WHAT DID YOU DO?" Is screamed at me in rage, but everything that I've done tonight is finally settling in and I'm feeling numb so I just shove her past her, throwing over my shoulder, "I did what I had to!"

Ethan meets us a few steps later and takes Jackson's weight off of me leaving my hands free to finish up what needs to be done with the commands. I use the tablet to send the orders for AIRIA to open the main barracks doors but to continue to keep every other door on lockdown. The soldiers will have only one option to exit the building, straight into the cleared area. That means we need to get out of here, quickly. I scream at the shocked faces around me to "MOVE!", causing some of them to flinch but it has the desired effect to get them running towards the truck.

Less than a minute later, the overhead doors open at my command and we're pulling out with Lance behind the wheel. I look over to check on Jackson, but it causes my heart to clench in sorrow at the pain he's going through right now so I look away and ahead. We have to go slowly over the rugged track with the livestock trailer attached to the back of the truck. I start pulling on one of my curls in nervousness that we're running out of time. If enough of the soldiers get in front of us and block the gate I don't know if Lance would plow ahead or stop.

A few minutes later, I feel a surge of relief when we swing around the side of the mountain and see the road between us and the gate is empty. There isn't even anyone standing at the gates guarding it anymore. We pass the row of trucks that won't be going anywhere, parked up against the rock wall, before clearing the edge of the mountain and getting a clear view of where the tents are set up. There are soldiers everywhere milling around. Some are fighting and some are on the ground rocking back and forth with grief but almost as one all heads turn our way when they hear the sound of our engine.

I yell out at Lance, "Floor it! Don't let them get between us and the gate to stop us!"

We're all thrown back against our seats as the big heavy vehicle surges ahead when he slams on the gas. The chain link gate might as well be tissue paper at how easily it parts when he hits it. He keeps the speed up as much as he can on the dirt track down the side of the mountain but thankfully it's fairly smooth after so much traffic has gone up and down it in the past week. As soon as we turn onto pavement he gets the speedometer back up again and throws a look at me over his shoulder.

"How long until you think they'll come after us?" he asks.

I shrug one shoulder, suddenly beyond exhausted. My voice is hoarse when I tell him, "They can come after us all they want but they're not going to catch up to us on foot. None of them will be driving. All the keys are locked inside in the armory."

He spares another glance over his shoulder and asks, "Are you sure?"

Sarcasm creeps into my tone. "What do you think?"

Marsh lets out a loud Rebel yell and leans over the seat behind me to wrap an arm around me. "I think you're a freaking superhero genius. That's what I think!"

I gently push his arm off of me and slump against the door. I'm not ready to celebrate yet. I'm well aware that there are two people in this vehicle that probably hate me right now. We drive into the night, stopping first to drop off Ethan and Marsh at Skylar's dad's truck. When it starts up and they pull in behind us we continue on our way to the highway. As we take the exit that leads to our new home, I remember there was another thing I wanted to do before we disappeared. We're not going to be able to accomplish it tonight because there are only three people here who actually know how to drive and two of them are already driving while the third is practically comatose. I lean forward anyway to tell Lance so that I don't forget.

"As soon as possible, we need to get over to the fields where they started the planting and take at least one of the tractors they left there. We will need it to do our own planting if we want to get enough in the ground to get us through the winter. It's essential."

I see him nod his head so I leaned back and slump once again against the door, staring out the window and up at the stars that have been hidden for so long. I don't know what's going to happen next or how long we will make it here, but at least we have a fighting chance now of rebuilding the right way.

I close my eyes and picture the two people who took me into their home and showed me what love was. I picture them smiling at me in pride for what I've done, for avenging them. Then, I let them fade away.

Chapter Seventeen...Skylar

I finish digging the hole under the only tree inside the camp's wall. Although it looks gray and dead I know there's life in it because tiny green buds are starting to form on its branches. In a few months, they'll grow into leaves and throw shade over this resting place. I toss the shovel to the side and kneel down picking up a jewelry box we had scavenged from one of the gift shops in the resort next to us. I gently lift the lid and look down at what I'm burying today. It's simply a piece of plastic, a completely lifeless object but it represents so much to me.

Not that long ago this plastic box could give me the sound of my mother and father's voices telling me that they love me. It could answer any question I asked of it when I was confused, lost or lonely. It represents seven years of me learning how to be an adult, how to be a mother, how to survive in this new world.

As I bow my head, I hear the sound of my little brother giggling with all the joy of freedom while he runs across the just greening grass that is growing here for the first time in so many years.

It's time to let go of the past and look to the future. There's so much opportunity for us here and it's thanks to this small square of plastic communicator that I'm ready for it.

I gently set the open jewelry box into the hole and reach out to close the lid but a soft sob escapes from my chest at saying goodbye. I hold back the next one that wants to come out, determined to put this behind me and reach out once again to close the lid. A green light flares awake on the front of the communicator and a tinny voice comes out of it.

"Skylar Ross, are you in distress?"

I rock back on my heels in surprise and wonder and the hole that I felt inside my chest feels a little less empty. I scrub the tears from my cheeks as a grin tugs at my lips but I continue the motion of closing the box. I grab the small shovel and cover the jewelry box with dirt and then pat it down firmly. I feel a sense of security knowing that my AIRIA will always be there if I need her but as I turn away and join Ben in a game of tag under the sun I know that I don't need her…for now.

Sign up to my newsletter to be notified of new releases and special discounted prices.

Please visit:

http://www.theresashaver.com/

Also by Theresa Shaver

The Stranded Series

Land – A Stranded Novel

Alex, Quinn, Josh, Cooper, and Dara - setting out on foot with nothing more than some soon to be worthless cash and a little advice from a trusted teacher, they walk through a burning city that has come to a halt. The devastation they see as they make their way out of the city is a small part of the horror that the nation will become. As the days go by with no food deliveries and no water flowing from taps, civilization will start to crumble and it will be survival of the fittest. With five States and half a Province to cross they will need to plan well, count on each other and pray for a little luck. Even with that, chances are slim of getting home when you are Stranded.

Sea – A Stranded Novel

Emily and her friends head to the California coast to find a boat back to Canada. They all felt that it would be much easier and quicker to sail home rather than go over land. They were wrong. Not only will they have to fight their way through the lawless city and the terrifying ocean, they will have a journey of hardship and loss as the biggest threat will come from within their own group. The trip home will change them all for good and bad as they are stranded at SEA.

Home - A Stranded Novel

Five went by Land and five went by Sea. Nine made it through the chaos Home. With their town under siege, and their families both prisoners and slaves, they will have the biggest challenge yet. After witnessing the pain and suffering in the town, the group of teens has to decide just how far they are willing to go to save them. Life sucks when you are Home, but still Stranded.

City Escape – A Stranded Novel

Mrs. Moore and the rest of the students that remained in California face the harsh reality that no one is coming to help them. As the city burns around them, they are surrounded by 18 million people with one goal…survival. Will Mrs. Moore's determination be enough to save them? Surrounded by chaos, they must work together to find a shelter before it's too late.

Frozen – A Stranded Novel

When the teen's town is hit with a devastating virus, they take it upon themselves to travel first to the closest military encampment to find the medicine their loved ones so desperately need. Stonewalled at every turn they make the hard decision to embark on an epic journey to a faraway city to search the ruins for help they need.

Traveling through a Frozen wasteland, they not only have to fight the elements and other survivors but also the inner struggles and changes each one has to accept and live with. It's not just the weather that has Frozen.

The Endless Winter Series

Snow and Ash – An Endless Winter Novel

Bomb after bomb dropped across the globe sending the world into a seemingly never-ending nuclear winter.

Skylar Ross is ten that day when she's ripped from dance classes and sleepovers to being an orphan in a prepper's paradise of a mountain bunker. Her determination to protect her baby brother keeps her locked away with nothing but responsibility and loneliness. Her father's words are a continuous echo, "Trust no one. Help no one."

Rex Larson is eleven that day. He's left stranded on the side of the road in a strange place far from home when his mother dies that first day. With his own small brother to look after, he is lost and alone. Rex has no choice but to trust complete strangers with his and his brother's future.

Two different survivors in two different circumstances spend the next seven years trying to survive until an explosive meeting changes both their courses and lives forever. Trust is almost impossible when you spend your whole life in the SNOW & ASH.

Rain and Ruin – An Endless Winter Novel

A hailstorm of bombs has blasted the world into a nuclear winter. The survivors have now spent seven long years in the snow and ash scratching out a lonely, hard existence.

Although comfortable in her safe and supplied bunker, Skylar Ross longed for more of a life than what she has. She thought she found it when she rescued Rex but the evil that followed him inside her home threatened the one person she holds most dear. Can she put aside her mistrust of others and give him and his people a second chance?

Rex Larson fell hard for Skylar and was excited about his group joining her in the safety of her bunker until he was betrayed by one of his own. Exiled back out into the cold, he prays that Skylar will change her mind.

Forced to flee the town when a deadly gang moves in, the survivors huddle in the cold hoping the gang won't find them and for Skylar to change her mind. When the weather turns for the first time in seven years, they don't know if it means the earth is starting to heal or if it's just more ruin.

Made in the USA
San Bernardino, CA
04 May 2018